The Last Kings

The Last Kings

C. N. Phillips

www.urbanbooks.net

Urban Books, LLC
97 N18th Street
Wyandanch, NY 11798

The Last Kings Copyright © 2016 C. N. Phillips

ISBN 13: 978-1-62286-780-6
ISBN 10: 1-62286-780-7

First Trade Paperback Printing September 2016
Printed in the United States of America

10 9 8 7 6 5 4 3 2

This is a work of fiction. Any references or similarities to actual events, real people, living or dead, or to real locales are intended to give the novel a sense of reality. Any similarity in other names, characters, places, and incidents is entirely coincidental.

Distributed by Kensington Publishing Corp.
Submit orders to:
Customer Service
400 Hahn Road
Westminster, MD 21157-4627
Phone: 1-800-733-3000
Fax: 1-800-659-2436

Prologue

Mocha

Motivation. It was just another word that held nothing but a dictionary definition to me. I stood in the mirror of a sleazy hotel bathroom staring into the dirty mirror above the white marble sink. Staring back was a woman with wide, light brown eyes that might have been pretty had it not been for the smeared mascara and bags under them. The long black hair, once neatly in place, was now disheveled. The red lipstick on my lips faded. I could barely recognize myself.

What am I doing? I thought to myself before grabbing a fistful of my thick hair.

I stood there in my matching black lace lingerie set; the sexiest that I could afford. The curves on my twenty-two-year-old body stood out, and although I was tired, the beauty in my round face did too. I heard my client snoring lightly in the other room. I always worked them out and put them to sleep; that way, it was easier to collect my money and sneak out the door. This night was different, however. I wanted to look at myself. Not just look, actually *see* myself. *In* the act, not the aftermath of designer shoes, clothes, and purses. So after the deed was done with my client, that was exactly what I did. I looked at the woman in the mirror . . . and hated her. I hated me.

I reached and grabbed a cigarette out of the box of Newports that the man had left on the sink in the bathroom and the lighter next to them. I could feel my stomach churning and knew that my body needed something to stomach my reflection. It was sad seeing myself like that, especially knowing that at one point in time, I was on top of the world. Shaking my head, I sighed. Although my appearance was disgraceful, there was one thing I knew for certain: I was going to go collect my money. I took a few hits of the cigarette before putting it out on the sink, leaving a circular burn mark. I didn't care; it wasn't my bill. I then quietly opened the bathroom door and tiptoed to the end of the bed where my cream-colored minidress lay. I slid it on as quickly as I could and slipped my high black pumps onto my feet.

My money had been left on the dresser before anything went down that night because I always had to see my money up front. Two thousand dollars for one night with Mocha, and trust me, it was *always* worth it. I looked disgustedly at the plump white man lying on the motel bed before snatching up my Gucci clutch and my money. I didn't know how much longer I could do what I was doing. I left the cheap room feeling like even less of a woman than any of the other times. I walked a little way to my all-black 2015 Chevy Impala SS. Getting in, I was relieved to finally be on my way home, even though that wasn't any better than that nasty hotel. Still, lying in *my* bed sounded good.

I was what some called a prostitute or a whore. I hated those names, but it was what it was. What I did was dangerous, but my clientele weren't just random thugs off the streets of Detroit. They were rich men, some married and others just lonely. The guy this night usually took me to high-class penthouses and suites, but tonight, he wanted to try a different fantasy. He wanted to "fuck me in a cheap hotel like the dirty little black whore I was." Whatever. As long as he was paying me. My money was top priority. Two thousand only got my clients an hour. Only sex if they didn't drop an additional two more stacks on top of the hourly rate. As you could see, he was one of my lower-paying customers.

The drive to my shabby neighborhood didn't take too long, and surprisingly, the streets of Detroit were silent this night. I rode with my windows slightly cracked so that I could feel the light breeze of the night on my face. No music played at all. It was just me and my thoughts. I drove by a few young boys patrolling the block ready to make a sale, if need be. I smiled sadly because deep down, I missed that life. The fast-money lifestyle with no dignity lost. I guess there was still a little speck of a hustler in me, although it had subsided over the last year since the brutal murder of my best friend, Sadie. Since I'd been out of the game a lot had changed. For one, I'd become a prostitute so the quick money and respect I was used to faded. Sometimes I hated myself so much because I didn't know how to make it without her. She had been the leader since we were kids, the mastermind in all that we did, and I missed her.

We were freshmen at a local college when we figured out that what we wanted school couldn't give us: never-ending money and power. At first a drug cartel was just a little joke between us, but then Sadie's big cousin Ray came to us on some Ace Boogie-type business. Ray had come across an Italian connect by the name of Vinny who could provide never-ending business. Sadie was down instantly, but I, on the other hand, was a little skeptical. Sadie, of course, talked me into it and before I knew it, we were on and getting it in big time. It was scary at first because being a girl in the game was like a person swimming in a pool full of hungry sharks. Yet, we started off big time, so it wasn't hard maintaining a leveled position where the top began. Ray then got us our first pistols.

"Niggas hate seeing a come up," he'd said. *"Especially when they're looking for one."*

His words held true because less than a week later, I had to use my .48, Lucy, for the first time. Somebody must have gotten wind of our operation because we were set up. That night, I killed somebody. I actually think I killed a few people. After taking my first life, I finally gave in. One way in, and one way out was how Sadie and I saw it. We were about that life as soon as we had made our first sale; it was money over everything in the beginning. The money rolled in, and our team got larger. In less than a year, we had the biggest drug operation Detroit had ever seen. Nobody was touching us. Not even the feds. Our operation was so underground, they didn't know who to trail. Sadie and I dropped out of school when we were twenty and moved in with Ray. Everything was going great . . . until I made the dumbest mistake somebody in my seat of power could do. I fell in love. Like Ray said, *"Niggas are always looking for a come up."*

I was so blinded by my heart that I didn't see what Khiron was doing until it was too late. Until he got what he really wanted: to be on top and to control our empire. He wanted everything Sadie and I had worked for, and unlike the boss that I was supposed to be, I was caught slipping.

Another thing Ray was known for saying was *"All your niggas ain't loyal."*

The Last Kings was betrayed by someone who should have been their most loyal. I remember seeing Khiron's bullet enter Sadie's body . . . her choke on her own blood until she died. Right there in front of me. Ray was next.

"You, Mocha, aren't going to get the luxury of death," Khy had said to me.

I would never forget those words. Every day after that I wished he would just kill me. Most nights I came home he was there waiting for me, even though we didn't stay in the same house. I was his trophy piece. His way of showing the world that he'd brought down the best. He was the king of our cartel; nobody was even coming close to him. Little did he know his plan was flawed because he hadn't thought it through completely.

See, Ray had been planning on getting out of the game. Calling it quits; he had enough money stacked up. He'd told one of us the information about his connect and that one wasn't me. Surprise, surprise. That put a slight dent in Khy's plan, especially when the Italians pulled business and went ghost. At first, things were shaky, but eventually, Khy found his own connect, and so far, the streets were taken care of.

Khy was a demon. I hated him. I sold my body at night just so I could stack up my paper to get away from him. Far away. There was nothing left in Detroit for me because he had, or took away, every single thing that had given me joy.

He moved me back into the hood to keep an eye on me while he lived like royalty in a mansion on the good side of town. I had a nice car, nobody bothered me, he paid all of my bills, and I didn't have any worries. That's what he told me constantly. He wouldn't even let me go back to school and get a semi-fresh start.

"Bitches like you belong at home in the kitchen or on their knees for they man," he said when I brought the subject up.

Khy changed from the charming man that I first knew. I take that back, I never knew that man. I met his game face. I know him now, though, and he had hell to pay.

Coming up on my home, I slowed to turn into the driveway of my one-story brick house. A shadow on my stoop caught my eye, and I could see that there was a person posted up, as if they were waiting.

"Who the fuck is that?" I said aloud to myself, unbuckling my seat belt.

It couldn't have been Khy. He had a key. The person stood up when I opened my door. Although it was dark out, I could make out the frame of a woman. At first, I thought she must be a crackhead looking for a hit, but the closer I got, I knew she couldn't have been. She was in designer clothes and heels.

"Excuse me, but who the hell are you? And why are you outside of my house?" I asked bluntly, putting my hand in my purse.

I wasn't scared. Lucy was in my Gucci, loaded and ready to bust. The stranger stepped down the three steps from my stoop toward the light by my garage door. Her features became more distinguished as the shadows no longer concealed her. I opened my mouth to speak again, but I caught my breath, and my heart became a drummer in my chest. The woman before me looked different than I remembered; her hair was in a bob cut. But the sharpness in her dark brown eyes were the same, and she was still gorgeous with her five-five frame and Coca-Cola shape. I couldn't believe it. I took a deep breath.

"Sadie?"

Chapter 1

Three Years Earlier

"Mocha, wake your lazy ass up!" I yelled at my best friend who was snoozing loudly in her bed.

She continued snoring like she hadn't heard me, although I was pretty sure the people in the dorm room next to us had. I grabbed a pillow from my bed and hauled it across the room at her, hitting her dead in her pretty sleeping face. The expression it held when she was fully awake almost made me regret my actions.

"Sadie!" Mocha growled before she sat up and shot me the dirtiest look she could muster.

I laughed. I couldn't help it. Who could take a person seriously when they had slobber sliding down their face? Not to mention her hair was all over the place.

"Shut up, bitch, and go clean yourself up. We have class in an hour," I said back to her still grinning.

"I don't see anything funny! I was sleeping good!" Mocha complained, stretching.

"Clearly," I said sarcastically.

"Fuck you, Sadie. I'm not going to class. I'm tired." Mocha tried to throw the covers back over her.

"Well, if you weren't out fucking Antwan's ass all night, you wouldn't be tired!" I walked to her side of our dorm room and snatched the cover back. "Your ho ass should have remembered you had class in the morning."

Antwan was Mocha's newest male interest. He was a wannabe hustler who thought he was the man. Key word: "thought." I personally didn't see what she saw in his tall, black self; besides his perfect smile and smooth chocolate skin. Other than that, I saw nothing appealing about him. He attended a few classes at the community college in Detroit, Michigan, where Mocha and I went, and he must have laid the D on her something vicious. He had my girl's head gone.

"Girl, don't hate!" Mocha said, sitting up. "Just because your pussy is covered in cobwebs doesn't mean you have to rain on my parade!"

I rolled my eyes at her comment. She was completely wrong, and I let her know so.

"Bitch, my pussy has standards unlike yours—Mrs. Bust It Wide Open for anyone with a big dick." I threw some clothes at her. "And don't forget that the only reason we're even here is because of our scholarships. We don't have time to slack off. Here, I even picked out your outfit!"

I was already dressed in a purple Victoria's Secret pink hoodie and sweats with my light tan Uggs. My long, dark brown hair was pulled on the top of my head in a bun. I had picked out a similar outfit for Mocha, except hers was red. I loved how the pants accented the curves of my hips and plumpness of my behind.

"I fucking hate your ass." Mocha stood up with her clothes and headed for the bathroom.

I could tell she had just recently had sex by the way she was walking, yet trying to pretend her legs weren't sore.

"You got forty-five minutes!" I yelled as the bathroom door slammed shut.

Twenty minutes later, Mocha walked out of the bathroom looking like a shapely model. I had always been a little jealous of her figure. We both had curves for days, but her butt was a little pumper than mine, and her hips a little wider. I got more luck than she did in the chest department with my 36 C-sized breasts, while she couldn't even fit a C. Her creamy mocha latte-colored skin was silky smooth. She wore her long hair wet, crinkled, but pulled back in a tight ponytail. The way her hair was slicked back brought out the light green specks in her light brown eyes.

"Awe, boo!" I gushed at her natural beauty. "You so cute."

"Leave me alone, Sadie, I'm still pissed off at you." She was trying hard to hold back her grin.

"Whatever." I handed her designer Coach backpack to her. "Let's go before we're late."

Mocha put on her matching Uggs, and we grabbed our pea coats, mine black and hers gray. I locked our room up and just like that, we were on our way. I made small talk on our way to our math class, mainly to keep my mind off of the cold nipping away at my ears.

"Have you talked to Ray?" I asked Mocha, swerving to miss a young white guy riding his bike on the tiny campus grounds.

"Bitch, he's *your* cousin," Mocha said through chattering teeth as she walked. "You'd hear from him before I would!"

I rolled my eyes at her smart remark, mainly because it held truth to it. Although my grandmother had taken Mocha in when she was fifteen after her dad was murdered and her mom ran off with the first man who would take her, she wasn't my blood. Ray looked at her like his little cousin, but he and I were closer. It hadn't felt like it the last three or four months, though. It seemed like he was distant. He set Mocha and I up with everything designer and kept our pockets full, but that still didn't make up for the absence of my favorite cousin. I knew that his name was loud in the streets, and I also knew what he did to keep it that way so it was something that I had to deal with. Knowing him, though, he would pop up sooner or later. We had almost made it to the building our class was in when we heard a deep voice and footsteps coming up behind us.

"God knows he's wrong for giving y'all all that ass!"

I whipped my head around ready to curse whoever it was. I calmed down when I saw it was nobody but Antwan's black self.

"You're so stupid," I shot him a dirty look.

"Antwan, it's too early." Mocha tried to sound annoyed, but I could tell she was a little happy at just the sight of him.

I couldn't lie, Antwan was looking fresh with his hair newly cut, and he was rocking Ralph Lauren head to toe. But still, he was so not my type. He licked his lips hungrily at Mocha while his eyes traveled her body up and down.

"Yeah, it's too early," Antwan caught up and began walking in between us. "What are the two baddest bitches on campus even doing up right now?"

"I'm not a bitch," Mocha snapped. "And we have class, silly; this is a school. Why the fuck else would we be up?"

Antwan chuckled and shook his head.

"Yeah, this is a school, and you obviously didn't check the school Web site either. If you're not an upcoming graduate, you ain't got school all week. Somethin' about neighborhood violence or some shit."

Mocha stopped in her tracks and glared at me.

"Fuck!" I said, remembering I had seen that the night before. "I forgot!"

"Fuck is right! Because I'm about to fuck you up!" Mocha told me.

"Damn, I said sorry!"

"When? I didn't hear it!" she huffed.

I wanted to punch her, but she was right. It was my mistake.

Antwan was cracking up.

"Aye, man, y'all are a trip! I'm going to fuck with y'all later though," he said and continued walking.

"Where are you going?" Mocha inquired.

"I got some business to handle," he said. "Aye, Sadie?"

"What's up?" I asked wondering what on earth he could have to say to me.

"My man C. J. wants to know what's up with y'all."

"Not a damn thing!" I informed him sternly.

C. J. was Antwan's best friend, who Mocha talked me into going out with. Whereas C. J. was sexy as he wanted to be and had a big dick to back it up, after a few dates and him discussing nothing but himself and money, I just couldn't do it. Also, after our third date, I actually let him come into my dorm so we could get it in. I was disappointed when he couldn't even last two minutes—and we tried *two* times! The whole situation made me mad because I didn't give myself to many people, and when I did, it usually was worth it. I stopped answering his calls after that, and he hadn't stopped trying to get at me.

"Damn! It's like that?" Antwan laughed loudly.

"Yeah, it's like that! Tell him when he can last longer than two minutes, his bitch ass *still* won't have a chance with me!"

"All right, I feel you, ma," he said and gave us two fingers to tell us good-bye.

"I cannot believe your ass has me out in the cold, and we don't even have class!" Mocha kept saying the whole way back to our dorm room.

Once there, she climbed right back into her bed after throwing off her coat and shoes. I sat down on my colorful polka-dot comforter and looked at my best friend.

"I'm sorry, Mocha; you know I wouldn't have woke your crazy ass up if I would have remembered we didn't have class today. That was a waste of both of our time."

"Fuck that. Even if we did, you shouldn't have woke me up. I'm tired of this shit," she said snuggling back under her covers.

I knew exactly what she meant. About a week ago, Mocha and I had a discussion after her school trip to Atlanta on the reason why we were in school in the first place. What we wanted to be when we graduated. Neither of us had an answer. We both made good grades, but we both had always hated school. If it hadn't been for my grandma Rae, we probably would have dropped out at the drop of a dime. We lucked up and got scholarships at the community college where we resided in Detroit. Grandma Rae made us go, and we only stayed because of the fat refund checks we got every semester. Mocha was a math genius, like Ray, and I excelled in English. That night she returned, we talked about using our refund check money to start our own little business. Mocha jokingly made a statement about starting a drug cartel. It was crazy because with all of the knowledge I had about it, I never thought about getting into the game myself. Mainly because every single one of the men my mother dated were hustlers who met sticky endings no matter how much of a boss they were. One of the worst experiences in my life happened due to the game and the life that came with it. After that, I was skeptical about that idea, and it made me worry about Ray every day. However, if it came down to it, though, I know I would be down for the ride.

"Really, Mocha, I feel you," I said lying back on my bed. "This shit is getting played out to me too. If I didn't think Grandma Rae would flip, I would have been gone."

"I know. These petty-ass refund checks can't cover the kind of taste I have. I'm tired of Ray buying all of our shit.

One day, he isn't going to be here, and school isn't taking me anywhere. I need to figure out what I'm going to do with my life. Right now, I feel as if I'm wasting it taking tests to get a degree that I don't even want."

"We can get jobs," I said but instantly took it back. I couldn't picture either of us flipping anyone's burgers. "Never mind."

"Right. The working world ain't for us," Mocha agreed, turning to face my bed.

"Yeah," I concurred.

There were a few minutes of silence before Mocha began speaking, a little more quietly that time.

"So you haven't talked to Ray at all?"

"No," I told her. "I don't know what's been up with us lately. I used to talk to him every day."

"Yeah, you know what they're saying, right? About Coopa?"

I nodded my head. Coopa was the kingpin of Detroit. He usually kept his business tight. From what I heard and saw, he was a man that you didn't want to cross. He shot first and didn't ask or answer any questions. He was a good-looking man in his late thirties; light skin with small brown eyes and well respected in the game. He currently was the head of the biggest drug trafficking operation the city of Detroit had ever seen, and his team consisted of all the hustlers in Detroit. Ray was like his right-hand man, which meant that Ray was big. Lately, though, I'd been hearing that some people wanted Coopa's head on a stick. Something about he had been making some business deals and not holding up his end of the bargain. He thought he was untouchable, and so far, he had been. I just didn't want Ray in any mess behind Coopa's messiness.

"What do you think about it?" Mocha asked me.

"I mean, what can I say? Ray's a grown-ass man. I just hope that when Coopa goes down, Ray doesn't go with him," I told her.

"Maybe he's just waiting for the right time to get out," Mocha threw out.

"Naw, Ray loves his life too much. If anything, he would just take over. Then we could finally drop out of this bitch," I said.

"What does that mean?" Mocha asked.

"Nothing," I said, not really knowing what I was saying.

"Sadie, are you really thinking about that?" she asked. "I thought we were just playing around with that shit."

"That 'shit' would be better than just sitting here wasting my life away doing nothing," I told her.

"You tripping; you're trying to be on some crazy shit," she said.

"Some C. N. Phillips-type shit," I said glancing at my bookshelf.

"OK, Say," Mocha said, calling me by my nickname. "This isn't a book! This is real life! Let's be real for a second. If we start up our own business, it would get shut down before we even took flight! Antwan told me about what Coopa did to those niggas from California. Their bodies were found in Dumpsters. Fuck with that shit if you want to, Sadie, but it's not smart. What makes it worse is that we're girls! You know what happens to girls in the game."

Mocha's rant went in one ear and out the other. I wasn't scared of Coopa. He was just a man who stood behind his army instead of in the front.

"Whatever, Mocha." I didn't feel like arguing with her, especially since she had been the one to even bring it up.

"For real, Sadie, do you think they would take us seriously?" she asked. "I mean, we don't know anything about the game to even try to play."

"*You* don't know shit about the game, Mocha," I said, and I thought about the question.

I knew the city was hungry, but I also knew that even though Coopa was running shit, he wasn't handling business like he should have been. Eventually, Detroit would birth a new king . . . so why not make it a queen?

"I don't know, Mocha. Maybe, but only if we were strapped heavy and had a team of loyal ones," I finally answered.

Mocha sighed heavily.

"I'm going to sleep. Your ass is crazy. I can't believe we are even still having this conversation."

I heard her turn over, and I lay facing the ceiling for a few more moments, lost in my own personal thoughts. If I could come up with a way to take the game by storm, I'd do it in a second. I'd grown up around the world of drugs and fast money. The attraction that I had to it was undeniable. It enticed my soul. I was ten when my mother dated her first hustler. My mother always had a new man almost every six months. They gave into all of her lavish wants and always made sure I had everything that I needed. My mother wasn't just your typical beauty; she was drop-dead gorgeous. Her father was part Dominican so her hair flowed almost to her butt. She didn't believe in the working world, so she played off of her wide hips and plump breasts because it worked for her. We moved around a lot, and in every city, she would date the new "big thing," until he either got himself killed or incarcerated.

The longest relationship she had was for two years, and I hated him. His name was Nino, and I was fourteen at the time. I was just coming into my looks and many would often tell me I was beautiful, just like my mother. My mother moved us into his large six-bedroom estate and promised me that "this was it." Like a fool, I believed her, like I always did. It didn't take long for the fairy tale to be shattered. Soon my mother began to realize that Nino was an angry and very possessive woman beater. Whenever my mother did anything he didn't agree with, he would floor her. For a while, my mother put up with it saying that she needed him, and if it wasn't for him, we would be on the streets. But when Nino started paying inappropriate attention to me, things started to really get out of control. Instead of protecting me like a mother should have, she turned to drugs. The same ones Nino was selling to the crack whores roaming the streets. The first night Nino raped me, he put a gun to my head and told me that if I screamed, he would blow my and my mother's heads off.

I had never felt pain like that before in my fourteen years, and I felt lower than dirt. He was large, too large for a young girl's first time. I remember biting my lip so I wouldn't scream. My womanhood was stripped from me in thirty minutes and fifteen seconds. I knew that because I'd closed my eyes and counted to mentally evade Nino as he humped my body deeper and deeper into the mattress. No matter how much of a failure my mother was, she was still my mother, and I didn't want him to hurt her any more than he already had. After that first time, it began happening periodically. I never spoke a word of it to my mother. Whenever she looked at me, her eyes reeked with sadness and pain. I could tell she knew what was happening, and the fact that she didn't do anything to stop it turned my heart cold. She was too strung out from playing with her nose to help me. She had completely lost her shape, and any beauty once in her face was long gone.

After some time, Nino actually began using me to make drops and collect his money. I used to take the drugs to school. When my beeper went off, I knew a customer was out front. Not the smartest idea in the books, but I never got caught, so it worked for me. Nino knew how much he would get back so I started to up the prices on my own so that I could make my own profit and give him what he knew he would get. If there was one thing being my mother's daughter taught me, it was to never depend on a man to take care of me. I saw how far that got her and made a promise to myself that I would never be in that position.

Nino had a son that lived with his mother, and he flew out often to see him, leaving my mother and me at peace. I remembered the last time he flew out to see him was the day after he had raped me so brutally that I bled all over the sheets. I decided then that I wasn't going to spend the rest of my life as his sex slave and flunky, so I snuck into his office. I hoped that I could find something in there to get him caught up, and sure enough, I did. It seemed that Nino, much like Coopa, had been making some bad business moves and owed a few people money. I made a few calls with the numbers I found, and when I was done, all I had to do was play the waiting game. It didn't happen right away, but I knew it wouldn't. I had a few more horrible nights when Nino came back, but it was all worth it as soon as I heard the front door being kicked in. At the time, my mother and I were in the kitchen eating our dinner when she heard the door cave in. The first thing she did was grab me and make a dash to the upstairs part of the house.

"What the fuck, Camara?" Nino screamed at my mother when we burst into the room they shared.

"They found us," my mom said in a hurried, hushed tone. "They just kicked in the door. We have to go, now!"

Nino jumped up, grabbing his gun before running to shut the door behind us. I could tell by the look in his eyes that he was terrified. We heard the people under us ransacking the house and knew it would only be a matter of time before they found us.

"But how did they find me?" Nino asked himself, trying to think of how they found his house.

I knew his mind was trying to find a solution. His house wasn't even listed; he had done that as a safety precaution, knowing his head was wanted on a few sticks. His eyes then locked with mine, and I couldn't help the devilish upward curl that formed on my mouth.

"It was you!"

Before he could grab me, the door flung open and shots rang out in the room. I will never forget seeing the shots enter into his body. That was the last sight I saw before my mother grabbed me and we fell back into the tall bookcase. In a matter of seconds, we were through the secret door and in another room. My mother was frantically grabbing already packed suitcases and stacks of money. I had never seen my mom move that fast. I remember hearing the intruders yelling about fucking with "the boss's" money and how they had trusted Nino with the coke. Instead, he was snorting it with a bitch. There was a window in the room, and my mother told me to climb out of it and use the side railing to slide down to the ground. I heard one final gunshot, and my mother pushed me out of the window. Once we were both on the ground, we ran as fast as we could to her car, and as we drove away from the house, I looked behind me, only to see flames shooting toward the sky as it was being burned to the ground. We drove all the way to Grandma Rae's house, where she dropped me off, saying she needed to grab a few things. She never came back, and Grandma Rae legally adopted me.

I guess that's another reason why Mocha and I were so close. We were both abandoned by our mothers. I never told her the full story. No one knew, not even Ray. Finally, I decided to put my thoughts to the back of my mind and get a few more hours of sleep. I turned the lamp beside my bed off and lay in darkness until I finally fell asleep.

Chapter 2

I woke up to the sound of my phone ringing next to my head on my white fluffy pillow. I wasn't quick to answer it because I was wondering who the hell was calling me.

"Hello?" My voice sounded groggy when I finally accepted the call.

"What up!" I'd recognize that deep, suave voice anywhere. The one and only Ray. "I know your ass isn't still asleep at one o clock?"

"Don't 'what up' me!" I said suddenly wide awake. "Where the fuck have you been?"

"Chill! Get up. I'm about to pull up in five minutes. Tell Mocha to get up too. I know her ass is still passed out if you are."

I looked over at Mocha, whose mouth was hanging open. I laughed a little bit.

"I'm right, huh?"

"Shut up, Ray. You better have your gloves with you because when I see you, I'm beating your ass. Especially with the shit I've been hearing."

"Yeah, yeah. I'm here, come out."

I hung up, then proceeded to wake Mocha up.

"Mocha, get up, Ray's here." I shook her arm.

"Sadie, I am going to fuck you up! This is the second time you've fucked up my beauty sleep!" Mocha tried to swat me off of her, but I didn't let her arm go.

"Ray's outside, get up!"

"I wish you would just leave me aloooone!" she grumbled, putting on her boots and coat.

"Shut up. I know you don't want to be cooped up in this small-ass dorm room all day," I said, trying to hurry and get out to the car.

Even though I was mad at him, I was excited to see Ray. It had been too long. The money he sent us every week didn't make up for him being ghost. I'm glad Mocha and I were still dressed from earlier because it didn't take too long to get out of our dorm.

"Lock the door behind you," I told Mocha.

"*Naw*, I'm just going to leave it unlocked," she said sarcastically and locked the door. "Why is he picking us up?"

"I don't know," I answered honestly going down the one flight of stairs and once again out into the cold air.

I saw his black Cadillac Escalade parked not too far from the dorm's entrance and led the way avoiding big piles of snow. His tint was so dark I could barely see inside of the car.

"What's up?" Ray grinned at us when we made it to the vehicle.

"Hey, cousin!" I grinned right on back, getting in the passenger seat. I couldn't help it. Ray was so handsome, and his smile was contagious.

He had his long dreads hanging, and I could see his little goatee trying to come in on his chestnut-brown face. He was casual, wearing a Diamond Supply T-shirt and 501 Levi jeans. On his feet he wore his French Blue 13's. My cousin was fresh even when he wasn't. His dark brown eyes were identical to mine except his were sharper when looked into. He looked just like our Grandma Rae, which was why my uncle Thomas named him Raymond. He was like the big brother I never had. Ray was tall and had a muscular build. He had women falling at his feet, but he was paying too much attention to his money to take notice. To his enemies, Ray was lethal. He held his temper well, but you definitely didn't want to get on his bad side.

"Ray," Mocha said, hopping into the backseat, "you better take us to get something to eat!"

Ray gave her the side eye.

"What were you doing still asleep? It's the afternoon. No, better question, why the fuck weren't y'all in class?" He took his eyes off of the road to glance at me.

"Damn!" I exclaimed. "Feds-ass nigga! We didn't have class today." I looked behind me and cocked my head at Mocha. "Check him out, Mo. He's worried about our schooling, but we haven't even heard from his ass."

"Right!" Mocha cosigned, laughing.

"Yea, laugh if y'all want to, but don't try to turn this around on me, Say," Ray said. "You both know it would fuck with Grandma Rae's heart if she found out y'all were fucking off in school."

"Fuck school! I'm about sick and tired of this shit!" Mocha said in an exasperated tone. "Grandma Rae just might have to be mad at me, because I'm about to throw in the towel after this semester."

"Me too," I agreed.

Ray shook his head at us.

"Y'all tripping. You both saw how pissed Grandma Rae was when she found out I dropped out of college," he reminded us.

He was right; I had never seen Grandma Rae that upset in my life. But at the end of the day, it was what it was. No one forced her to go or stay in school, so why should I be forced to?

"Nigga, I just want to be on; fuck college," I said.

"Fuck college, huh?" he chuckled. "I feel you, though."

"Yup. I'm tryna be like you when I grow up. I just don't know why you hitting the block for a nigga that's losing to the game. The streets are talking."

"I don't work for Coopa. I work *with* Coopa. Fuck what the streets are saying. This is a business, and the only people who really know what the fuck is going on are the people *in* the business."

I rolled my eyes in a "Whatever" like fashion and looked out my window before the conversation went on any further. I noticed we reached a restaurant a few blocks away from Grandma Rae's house that I never even knew was there.

"Roll your eyes at me again and in a second, you're going to be lookin' like Beyoncé when she fell down them fuckin' stairs!"

I tried not to, but I started cracking up, thinking back to when I'd first seen the video. I loved me some Beyoncé, but only a person without eyes wouldn't think that fall was hilarious. I heard Mocha's high-pitch laugh join mine.

"Fuck you, Ray!" I said opening my door. "And you can't park for shit!" I noticed that he was slightly over the line in his slot.

Ray led the way to the little farmhouse-shaped restaurant. Once inside, the host led us to our seats, telling us our server would be right with us. We took off our coats and got comfortable in our chairs.

"How are your cars running?" he asked us.

Ray had also purchased Mocha and me matching BMW 128i coupes. Mine white, hers all-black. Nothing too flashy; just something to get us from point A to point B.

"They're good; I'm ready to be sitting on something big like you though!" Mocha beamed.

It was well-known that Ray had an array of vehicles. All paid for. He would always say he wasn't a predictable guy. When he pulled up, most times you wouldn't even know it, but his truck was his baby. It was decked out with everything luxurious, and the complete outer layer was bulletproof.

He laughed, "Naw, y'all straight. Niggas like me need more than one car."

In that one statement he separated himself from the two of us. My cousin was paid. Period. He recycled cars like girls recycled panties.

"Bullshit," Mocha waved her hand at him. "A sexy girl needs a sexy car. One she can get around in the snow in!"

"Nah, Mocha, you just can't drive; don't blame the car," I joked, and she threw a balled up napkin at me.

"You two haven't been out here much, have you?" Ray asked, changing the subject.

"And if we were, I'm sure you would already know," I gave him a smug look.

It was hard having a life when your big cousin knew the whole city. Even if he hadn't seen us in forever, he would know about what we were doing and who we were doing it with. Ray tried to give us some kind of independence post-high school after we complained about having his goons with us at all times. But I knew that he never really gave in to that; he just made his goons unseen to our eyes.

"You're really like the fuckin' feds, Ray," Mocha shook her head. "Can't even get my cat scratched without your ass all up in my shit!"

The look on Ray's face said he wanted to reach across the table and wring her neck, but he played it cool. Mocha and I were the only ones besides Grandma Rae and Ray's best friend Tyler who spoke their minds to him, but we knew when to shut up. At the age of twenty-four, Ray was the type of man that, when he got mad, you ducked. With his six-foot-two frame and muscular build, I could see why many were intimidated by him.

Another thing about Ray that I admired was that no matter what he was wearing, he always carried the essence of money, such as that very moment. Eyes kept shifting to and from our table. Everyone knew who he was, but no one tried to approach.

Despite the type of business that he was in, Ray was actually very educated and could hold a conversation with anyone about anything. Grandma Rae was upset about him dropping out of school, but she stood by his decision. She knew what Ray was doing, but what could she do? Ray was a grown man in his own big house; he wasn't sheltered under her roof anymore. If Mocha and I followed in his footsteps, I knew it would break her heart. She wanted me to be some amazing doctor or something, but I knew that wasn't me. I eyed Ray from my side of the table and tried to gather my thoughts before I opened my mouth.

"How'd you find this place?" Mocha asked, looking around the restaurant.

The place was called All Or Nothing, and it was packed with people. The aroma was wonderful, and the design was very high end and classy. There were red booths against the walls of the square-shaped restaurant and black tables with red chairs in the middle. On the walls were replicas of famous framed paintings, and all of the help wore white-collared shirts, black pants, and red bow ties. I was completely unaware of such a nice restaurant in a bad neighborhood.

"I know the owner," Ray shrugged. "I gave him a little something to start the place, and ever since, whenever I come in, he hooks me up."

"Nigga, you know everybody!" Mocha shook her head.

"It's called *networking*; try it sometime," he said just as our waitress came to take our orders. "Speaking, of which, Mocha, how was your trip to Atlanta?"

Mocha looked slightly caught off guard, but it only lasted a split second.

"It was OK; it's not like I was there on vacation. We went to some bullshit-ass museum and looked at some dead muhfucka's remains," she mumbled, not really looking at him.

I couldn't help wondering why she was acting so strange suddenly. She didn't really speak about the trip to Atlanta she'd taken with her anatomy class; I just figured it must have been boring, and she didn't want to dwell on it. Mocha's face spelled relief when a pretty young waitress approached our table. Good thing too, because I was about to call her out.

"Hi, my name is Tammie, and I'll be your server today. First, can I start you off with some drinks?" she asked us while staring hard into Ray's eyes.

She was a cute chick, a little skinny, though. I was feeling her short haircut. Her hair was curly in an asymmetric bob with light auburn highlights.

"For us," I motioned toward Mocha and me, "lemonade, light ice. And for him, a Pepsi, cold but no ice, please." I knew them like the back of my hand and when she heard no complaints, Tammie wrote it down on her little notepad.

"OK, got it," Tammie said. "Are you guys ready to place your orders?" She smiled at Ray with eyes that said she hoped he wanted to place an order for her.

"Let me get two bacon cheeseburgers and a crispy chicken Caesar salad, if you don't mind," Ray smiled back at her.

"One of those burgers better be for me, Ray. You know I ain't fucking with no salad!" Mocha exclaimed, acting like her loud self again.

Our waitress laughed at her comment as she scribbled some more in her notepad.

"OK, I'll get this right out for y'all," and with one more flirtatious look to Ray, she went to put in our order.

"Damn, is she switching hard enough?" Mocha shook her head. "Bitches go crazy over you, Ray. I, personally, don't see it," she teased.

"Whatever," he waved her comment off. "These bitches just want somebody to save them, and I'm not that nigga. Especially after Shira's nasty ass."

"That dumb bitch." I got mad at the mention of her name.

Shira was Ray's ex who had faked a pregnancy with his baby. Long story short, I called her out on it, she got mad, and I broke her jaw. My outer layer may have been prissy, but I came up in the streets. Growing up with my mom and her men, seeing death and violence was nothing. I honestly had wanted to break more than just her jaw for trying to cash out on my cousin, but she dropped after one hit, so what could I do? Moral of that story was . . . Don't mess with my family. I guess she learned her lesson because her banged-up face was no longer seen in Detroit.

"Ray, make sure your dick is strapped at all times. These hoes these days have no morals," I told him seriously.

"Chill, Say!" Ray told me. "I'm not checking for a bitch right now. I'm all about my paper."

"That don't mean you aren't fucking them!"

Women were nasty. Too quick to try to trap somebody with money. I guess when it came down to it, I was as overly protective of him, as he was over me. Tammie came back with our drinks and confirmed that our orders should be out within a few minutes. I sipped my lemonade, and the three of us sat in silence for a few moments waiting for our food to arrive. When it finally did, we all dug in like we hadn't eaten in ages. I took a pause from eating and stared at Ray going to town on his burger. I knew the time was now or never.

"What?" he asked.

I figured then was a better time than any to ask him the question that I'd been dying to ask. I was going to butter it up, but I decided not to. Ray and I had always been straightforward with each other, and I wasn't about to change that.

"When are you going to put me on?" I just came out and asked like it was nothing.

As soon as the question was out of my mouth, the two of them stopped chewing their food abruptly. Mocha hadn't realized how serious I was until that very moment, and I didn't think she knew what to say. I hadn't warned her that I was going to bring the matter to Ray, but the anxious expression on her face as she looked at Ray awaiting his answer let me know she was on my side. I knew Ray hadn't expected that question either, but he regained his ability to speak quickly and wiped the surprise from his face.

"Shut up with that shit, Sadie. You don't know what you're asking for, shorty," Ray said, putting a fry in his mouth.

"Nah, for real, Ray. You think I'm playing?" I lowered my voice although the restaurant was very noisy. "I've been thinking about this for a while now. You think I would bring this up to you without thinking it through? I've done all my research on it. I lived the lifestyle for a long time, so I know what I'd be getting myself into. I just need you to say yes."

"That's funny," he scoffed. "I didn't know you could study to be a drug dealer. But since we're talking real shit, Sadie, let me be one hundred with you. They call this shit a game, but ain't nobody playing with it. One way in, and no way out. Everybody's not made out for this life, especially not my little cousins. So quiet that noise."

"Quiet what noise, Ray? You knew who my momma was, and the shit she was about. I was raised around it, so I guess you can say I'm already in it. Blood deep! You know this! I just need a connect and a starting point. And don't tell me what I'm cut out for, because niggas probably said the same thing about you. But now look at you."

"You don't get it, Say. From the outside looking in, shit looks all gravy. Seeing my pockets full and my whips, you would think it was easy. Nah. You have to be ready every second of every day to pull the trigger on a nigga. You have to come to terms with the fact that most niggas *ain't* loyal. It's more than them little niggas you see on the corners making those baby-ass moves. This is a business. This is about keeping the city happy. Everything goes hand in hand. Everybody eats, but to be all the way real, it's not too happy right now. It's not the time to take any new recruits."

"Because of Coopa? So why you working for him then?" I inquired, not quite getting where Ray was going with what he was saying.

"I already told you I don't work *for* that nigga. I work *with* him, but you wouldn't understand, Sadie."

"Enlighten me then, Ray!" I raised my voice a little.

"Sadie, not right now," Mocha lightly touched my leg.

I sighed and backed down, but I was not finished. Ray was confusing me. He was saying he didn't work for Coopa, he worked with Coopa. But if Coopa was king of Detroit, what was the difference? I reluctantly continued eating my salad so that I wouldn't say anything that I would regret later. I would have gotten up and walked out had it not been for the fact that I didn't drive my car.

"Say, look—" Ray started but was interrupted by the ringing of his phone. "Hello?" he answered.

"You OK?" Mocha asked me while Ray spoke into his phone.

"I'm fine," I lied.

"I just can't believe you were serious about this shit," she said to me, shaking her head.

Before I could reply, I heard Ray's voice get louder.

"What the fuck do you mean, nigga?" Ray was calm, but his tone held an underlying anger. His whole demeanor had changed in a matter of seconds.

Mocha and I exchanged confused looks as we continued listening to Ray's heated conversation.

"I'm on my way. When I get there, you better hope that shit reappears; otherwise, all y'all muhfuckas is dead. Ask y'all to do one simple fuckin' thing and you can't even do that. Does Coopa know?"

I heard the voice on the other end of the phone speaking quickly.

"Nah, fuck that shit, nigga. I keep y'all muhfuckas strapped. If Coopa's shit is gone, then that means y'all should all be dead. Period. I'm pulling up in five."

Ray hung up the phone, pulled out a hundred-dollar bill from the pocket of his Levis and dropped it on the table.

"Let's go."

"Ray, what's going on?" I asked trying to keep my pace with him in the coldness of the winter air. He ignored me and got in the truck. "Ray, what the fuck is going on?" I asked again.

"You want this life?" he finally answered, looking straight-ahead. "You want to be part of this game? I'm about to show you what happens to niggas who fuck up in it."

Chapter 3

Ray pulled up to a house about five blocks away from Grandma Rae's, and the car was silent when he stopped. The house wasn't much of a looker with the white paint chipping and the crooked brick stairs leading to the front door. In the driveway was a brand-new black Mercedes coup not even plated yet. It was a little dirty, because of the mud and snow on the ground. Ray parked behind it and got out of the car without a word to Mocha or me. I wasn't about to just sit in the car, so I hopped out after him. By the time Mocha got out of the car, Ray was already inside the house.

"What the fuck is going on?" Mocha huffed in my ear as we made our way to the door.

I just shrugged. I didn't know what was about to happen. But when I looked at Ray's face while he was driving, I knew something serious had gone down. We strolled through the door after Ray without knocking, and as soon as we entered, I felt as though I was walking into a crime scene. The place was trashed. The living room was right in front of you when you walked through the door; all the furniture was flipped over. The television screen had a big hole in it and was lying on its side. There was a big tan couch flipped at such a crazy angle, looking at it made me feel awkward. I felt and heard the crunching of glass as Mocha and I made our way to the back of the one-story house toward the kitchen. I knew whatever had happened hadn't been anything good, and listening to Ray's voice travel from the kitchen, I knew he wasn't happy.

When Mocha and I finally made our way to the kitchen, we saw four men standing before Ray. Fear read all over their faces, and anguish was all over Ray's. They were lined up in front of the refrigerator, and when we made our presence known their eyes shifted to us. We stood away to the farther right side, out of the way, to observe the scene at hand. Ray ignored the two of us and kept his eyes on the men in front of him.

"So what the fuck is up?" Ray put his hands in his pockets and shrugged his shoulders. "My man Jay here," he nodded his head at one of the light-skinned men standing closer to Mocha and I, "said y'all got hit a few hours ago. Everything is gone, is that right?"

Nobody dared to speak. Ray had them spooked, and to be honest, I was a little shook too. Ray's voice was low and calm . . . but deadly. His vibe controlled the temperature of the room, and the room was cold. He walked to one of the men to the far left end of the kitchen.

"What happened, Little?" he asked him.

Little's name fit him perfectly. He was short and dark skinned with big fat French braids in his hair. He blinked rapidly with Ray less than a foot away from him and seemingly tried to think of his answer.

"Man, Ray, those niggas just busted u-up in here. I don't know who the fuck been talking, but they knew this was a trap," Little's high-pitched voice stuttered.

"So you just let them take the shit?" Ray asked rhetorically.

"N-nah, man. They was strapped h-heavy, Ray—"

"Nigga, each and every one of you muhfuckas has a burner!" Ray barked, the calm gone from his tone. "Y'all weren't on your A-game if y'all let some niggas walk up in this bitch and take the shit! Just 'cause they had guns? Nah, something in this fucking story ain't adding up."

I inhaled sharply, not knowing what was going to happen next. Ray went to stand in front of the tall guy standing next to Little. The man ran his hand over his fade haircut and had to force himself to look at Ray.

"You and Shy ain't do shit either, huh, Tre?" Ray shook his head at the two caramel-skinned men in the middle. Both were rocking a fade haircut.

None of the men looked younger than twenty or older than twenty-five, but I would probably never know their ages. I heard Mocha's quick breaths beside me, and I wanted to comfort her, but I was too frozen in place.

"They would have killed us, man!" Tre tried to reason.

"Then y'all should have died!" Ray barked again. "All four of y'all are pussies, and you lack what we need in this business. Brains."

Ray then did something I wouldn't have expected at a time like that. He began laughing. Hard. He waved a finger at the four of them and shook his head.

"Enough with the games, though. I'm done entertaining the bullshit," he told them. "What's funny to me is that the only people who know about this house are Coopa, me, and you four. We are the *only* ones who also know when the product and money will even *be* in this bitch. So you know what I'm getting at, right?" He nodded his head at them. "One or all of you niggas is a snake. And I don't need any snake-ass muhfuckas on my team. Fifty stacks gone. Twenty bricks gone. I'ma just say this shit, you young niggas are bold as hell."

"Nah, man—" Jay tried to say.

"Shut the fuck up!" Ray got in his face, causing him to jump back. "When I lose money, it's not a good thing. But when Coopa loses money," Ray removed a 9-mm pistol from his waist, "niggas die."

My heart began to beat uncontrollably fast. I couldn't believe what I was witnessing. It was the first time I'd actually seen Ray on the job firsthand.

"Oh shit," Mocha breathed, grabbing my arm and trying to back us further into the kitchen wall.

"Now *what* the fuck really happened?" Ray asked screwing a silencer on his gun. "Jay, that's a nice Mercedes out front. Looks like you just came up on some money . . . or are about to."

Ray and Jay locked eyes, and there were a few seconds of silence. Out of the corner of my eye, I saw Shy and Tre reach for their hips but before they could even aim, I heard two small *spiffs*. Two round circles appeared in the middle of their foreheads, and the refrigerator behind them was sprayed with blood. Beside me, Mocha jumped but didn't make a sound.

"Ray, you know I wouldn't set no shit like this up!" Little pleaded like a little bitch.

"I don't know," Ray cocked his gun. "That's why all of you have to die. I'd rather be safe than sorry."

He fired again, and Little slumped. His eyes averted back to Jay, who was literally shaking where he stood. I watched the scene before me like I was at an opening at midnight for the latest comedy.

"Jay, Coopa put you in charge, nigga, and *this* is what you do? I know those niggas weren't smart enough to come up with no shit like this. What the fuck, man?"

"Ray," Jay threw his hands up. "Come on, bro, we boys!"

Ray smirked at his futile attempt at throwing their friendship into play.

"Boys?" Ray spat. "Nigga, we *ain't* boys."

"Man, all right, coo. But you and I both know Coopa ain't doing shit for the city. That nigga don't give a fuck about nobody but his fuckin' self. Not even the niggas out here in the streets every day putting in work for *that* nigga. Fifty bands ain't shit to him! He's sitting on millions, fuck him! I have to eat, son; got shit I have to handle. And since that nigga ain't giving, why not take? Ray, the streets are hungry, and they're talking."

"Talking?" It seemed that some of the things that Jay was saying sparked Ray's interest, although his gun never lowered.

"Yea, nigga. Talking. Muhfuckas don't like how Coopa been handling his business, even called his product bullshit. You know better than me, Ray. You know Coopa ain't doing right in the game."

"All right, Jay." Ray nodded. "I feel you on what you're saying and all, but who the fuck are you to take matters into your own hands? Robin Hood, nigga?"

"Real shit, Ray, everybody knows Coopa wouldn't be shit without you. That nigga would have been fell off if you weren't on his team. You should be running shit, not him. This money could be the start of ya' empire, nigga. And I would be on your team."

"First off, nigga, I know all of this. Second, I plan on being king sooner than later, but when it happens, why the fuck would I want a snake like you on my team? You're a smart nigga, though, just not smart enough."

"Ray—"

"Did you think I was stupid when you called me with that bullshit-ass story? As soon as I walked in this bitch, I smelled the lie in the air. Oh, and I saw that the board you dumb muhfuckas flipped the couch over was loose. This shit ain't nothing new to me. Sadie, go pull that shit up."

"W-what?" I asked. I had forgotten that they could see Mocha and me.

"Go pull that board up," he instructed again, never taking his cold eyes off of Jay.

I pried my arm away from Mocha and did as I was told. I walked back into the small living-room area, glass crunching under my feet, toward where the upside-down tan couch was. The one I saw once we entered the house. I used my body to scoot it to where I had access to the board underneath it, and sure enough, it was slightly lifted aloof from the other boards. I pulled it, and it easily broke away from the floor. Underneath it was a long black duffle bag and a metal suitcase. I grabbed both, even though they were a little heavy, and lugged them back into the kitchen. I dropped both in front of Ray and Jay but curiosity got the best of me. I knelt down and unzipped the duffle bag, revealing at least twenty bricks of cocaine wrapped neatly. I also opened the suitcase and saw more Ben Franklins than I'd ever seen up close in person. I stood back up and looked at Ray who locked eyes with me before looking back at Jay.

"Sadie, what do I always tell you and Mocha?" he asked me.

I saw his right arm rise, and I took a deep breath and whispered, "All your niggas ain't loyal."

I could still taste the words on my lips when one final shot rang out.

Chapter 4

A few weeks passed since the incident at the trap house, and Ray harbored some guilt for letting Mocha and Sadie see it go down. But because of what he was planning, he knew they had to see it. What he had in mind was big, and he needed to break them into the business somehow. Deep down, he did not want them to be part of the life that he lived every day, but to be honest, besides his best friend Tyler, they were the only other two people that he trusted with his life.

Ray was born and raised in Detroit, so he'd seen a lot of things; death, betrayal, and hatred. He'd rarely seen love or "real." Real niggas were a thing of the past, only to be replaced by clones of the real thing. Yet, everybody knew that nothing was better than the original. Ray wasn't raised around riches or fame, but once he got the money, he became accustomed to it. He was a hood celebrity, just like everyone major down with Coopa's operation. Sadie and Mocha were well-known as well; Tyler's younger sister Marie too. They were the princesses in the hood. There was a time where Sadie and Mocha couldn't even leave the house without five soldiers with them. With his name growing heavier in the streets, Ray knew they could easily be targets.

The two young women were so much alike, but so different. Sadie was well structured, and he'd always known she didn't want to go to school, but he agreed with Grandma Rae when she said that's where she needed to be. Sadie had something he didn't see in a lot of men. She had a "Go-Getter" attitude and could back it up tenfold. Ray trusted her with everything he had, and her position on his team was already solidified. Just like he leveled Coopa's mind, he knew Sadie would do that for him. She would keep him from making any messy decision that could potentially ruin the uprising of his operation.

Mocha was efficient; she was the type of person who could tell if something was out of place with one glance. Ever since she'd come to stay with them, he noticed how good with money she was. Counting it, flipping it, and doubling it. She was about it; Grandma Rae never had to give her a dime. He needed that on his team as well. Tyler was Ray's right-hand man. Tyler was a man who kept his brain in his trigger finger. Once you crossed him, you crossed him. He'd been bodying his enemies with his .45 since the age of eighteen. He didn't have a heart, and if he did, it only extended out to the four of them. *Kill or Die Slow*, that was the code that he lived by. He had to fight his whole life, and that fact made him the perfect general for The Last Kings.

The Last Kings . . . Ray had been repeating it in his head for the last few months of planning. He felt as if they were the last real ones in the world, and for that, they should be treated as royalty. The last of a dying breed. He knew from what the four of them witnessed growing up that they were strong enough to endure the hardships that came with the hustle. He knew right away that when brought to the table, Sadie would be down. He saw the look in her eyes when she saw all that money. He also knew that as long as Sadie was down for the cause, Mocha would be too. They were ride or die. He was just waiting for their call. What Jay had said about Coopa losing touch in the streets was more right than anyone even knew, but he had kept that information to himself as he plotted his takeover. He knew Coopa would soon fall off, but before that happened, Ray planned to be well on his way to the top. Never had Ray been a sneaky person, but business was business. He wasn't going to rob Coopa of anything the man had earned during his reign. He was just going to take Detroit by storm, and in no time, Ray was sure that the streets would be calling his name.

Not Coopa's.

Chapter 5

"Say, are you all right?"

My mind heard Mocha speaking to me but couldn't register her words. I was lost in my own thoughts, hoping they would fall into place. The only consistent thoughts were of the money in that duffle bag and the blood that had spilled over the kitchen. Ray handled the situation without breaking a sweat, and I couldn't help but to admire it. The power that he held and the money enticed me. Mocha hadn't said a word to me about it. It was like she was trying to put it in the back of her mind. Or maybe she was just waiting for me to bring it up. Either way, there was a strange aura in the air whenever we were together after the incident.

"Bitch, I know you hear me talking to you!" Mocha's voice was finally able to snap me out of my own head.

"Yea?" I rolled over on my bed to look at her. "What?"

"So you were just going to ignore me?" she said sitting, legs crossed on her bed.

"My bad," I said. "I was just thinking about some things. What did you say?"

"I asked your rude ass if you were OK. You've been acting different."

"I'm good, Mo. I've just been thinking, that's all."

"About what?" she asked just like I knew she would.

I shrugged my shoulders, but I knew she wasn't going to let it go that easy.

"About what, Sadie? Talk to me." She stood up in her sweats and came to sit on my bed beside me. I moved away from her a bit, not wanting her to touch me.

"Mo, chill. I've just had some things on my mind."

"Like?" Mocha pressed.

I knew she wasn't going to leave me alone until I told her the truth, so I did. Suddenly, I didn't care about what she thought. I took a deep breath and began speaking.

"I've decided that after this semester I'm dropping out of school. I might not even wait until then. College just isn't for some people, and I'm in that category. You know? And I think you feel the same way. I could stay, but what for? To make Grandma Rae happy? What about my happiness? I want *money*. And I want it now. Like *right now*. I mean, did you *see* that briefcase full of money, Mocha? All that currency. I'm trying to get like that. I feel that I can hold my own against any nigga without an army behind me. I've been around this shit my whole life. It's only right that I take my rightful place in the game. Then take the throne; or one of them."

When I was done, Mocha didn't say a word. Instead, she stared into my eyes, and I looked back wondering how much of an idiot she thought I was. When she finally did speak, there was something different in her voice.

"Sadie, there's a lot more that comes with that shit. People get put on every day and never make it to Coopa's level. Instead, they usually end up six feet under. You know, you watch the news just like I do. You know that these niggas are snakes, especially if they see a bitch getting paid big money. So are you sure you want to take a blind dive into this shit?"

I didn't even have to think about it.

"Rats are going to rat, and snakes are going to hiss. The game will never change, Mocha, and the potential danger doesn't scare me . . . It excites me. Shit makes me want to cum. I'm almost twenty years old, and I know this is what I want to do."

"How are you going to do it? Huh? Are you going to be out on the corners selling that shit yourself? So you can get bumped up by the feds?"

I could tell Mocha was getting frustrated, but I also could tell that she knew, like I knew, that my mind was made up. I shrugged my shoulders at her again.

"Ray got me," I answered her simply.

"Ray doesn't want you to live that lifestyle. Didn't you hear what he was saying?"

"No," I shook my head disagreeing with her. I thought about my cousin, I knew him better than anyone, even his best friend. "He wouldn't have let us see what went down if he was serious about me not being in the game." I saw a look of understanding spread across Mocha's face. "He was testing us, Mocha. Don't you get it? I don't know what Ray has planned, but you heard what that dude said about Coopa, and I could tell by Ray's face that it was true. I know my cousin; he's just waiting for me to call."

It took me a while to put two and two together, but I'd finally figured it out. Ray could have easily dropped Mocha and me off at our dorm before he went to handle his business, but instead, he took us with him. He wanted to see how we reacted to the cutthroat life he lived. He had always been like that, ever since I'd come to live with Grandma Rae. He was always testing me. But little did he know, I was ready. Mocha gave a long sigh and shook her head. Some of her curls hung loosely from her ponytail.

"OK, Sadie, if this is what you want . . . I'm down. But, bitch, if I die, I'm killing your ass."

Chapter 6

While Mocha was in her English class, I decided to pay my Grandma Rae a visit. I felt a little guilty, especially since I was planning to go against her wishes with my schooling, but I couldn't help the fact that I missed her. I always liked to check on her just to see how she was getting along being in the house by herself. I used the key she'd given me to enter her house, and, of course, I instantly smelled a wonderful aroma coming from the kitchen.

"Grandma Rae?" I yelled out into the one-story house, closing the door quietly behind me.

I took my coat off and put it on a hanger in the hallway closet. To my right was Grandma Rae's living room. It was nice size with black leather furniture sitting on the softest tan carpet. There was a black wooden table in front of the furniture, and the entertainment center was against the wall. Her flat-screen TV made the one at the dorm look like a baby. I kept straight, going toward the kitchen where the smell was coming from and saw a shadow bustling around in the light.

"Grandma Rae?" I called out once more.

"In here, chile!" she yelled back at me from the kitchen.

I entered the kitchen and saw my grandmother in a cute peach jogging suit outfit, an apron, and house slippers. Although she had silvery gray hair that fell just above her ears, Grandma Rae didn't have a wrinkle on her body. She had the high cheekbones of a runway model and sharp brown eyes just like me and Ray.

"Mmm! Grandma Rae, what you cooking?" I set my purse on the high six seating kitchen table and went to where she was over at the stove.

"Just some corn bread, macaroni and cheese, yams, and fried chicken," she told me wiping her hands. "You hungry, baby?"

"You know I am! Did you know I was coming over?" I said.

"I figured you or your hardheaded cousin would make an appearance," she said with a knowing smile.

My mouth was watering. She made me a plate, and I took it to the table to dig in. The first bite was pure perfection, and I didn't know how I was surviving without her cooking at the dorm. I knew everybody said their grandma could cook, but my grandma cooked as well as Whitney Houston sang. There was no one better. Her dream at one point in time was to open her own restaurant, but then she got pregnant and married a man who felt she would do better as a housewife. Whenever she spoke about her dreams and not being able to follow them, I always noticed the sadness in her eyes. I think that was why she wanted Mocha and me to go to school so bad, to make it and be something one day. I just wished I could live up to her expectations. I didn't have any dreams of a career, well, an honest career, that is. My dream was to lead the biggest drug cartel Detroit had ever seen. I wanted it all, and if I were to tell my grandmother that was the life I wanted to live, I was almost certain it would break her heart.

"What's wrong with you, girl?" Grandma Rae stood over me staring with a concerned expression. "You look like somebody stole your man or somethin'!"

"No, I'm fine, Grandma Rae," I laughed at her comment. "I was just focused on my food."

Grandma Rae gave me a skeptical look, but she left me alone.

"Where's that girl Mocha at? I barely ever see the two of you apart! Like two peas in a pod you two are," she said and sat down at the table with me.

"She had class, and I just was tired of being cooped in that dorm," I told her.

"Well, make sure you take that girl a plate. You know she loves my corn bread," she waved her finger at me.

"Her ass does too," I said under my breath, taking my last few bites of food.

"What?" Grandma Rae asked, not hearing what I said.

"Oh nothing," I told her. "How have you been, Grandma Rae? I see Ray is still keeping you fly."

"Yea, you know that boy loves spendin' his money on me." Then she shook her head and stood up to start cleaning the kitchen. "I keep tellin' that boy to save his money! Buying me all this designer shit. I'm sixty-five years old! What do I need Gookie for?"

"I think you mean Gucci, Grandma Rae." I giggled at her horrible pronunciation of the word.

"That's exactly why I don't need it!"

"You're right!" I said still laughing.

"I just wish he would settle down. When I don't hear from him, I can't help but to worry. I know what he does, and I don't like it, not one bit!"

I felt my head fall slightly; I couldn't look her in the face. I heard her sigh and continue sweeping.

"But he's grown now and has to find his own way. I know that money is addictive, but it's dangerous. Patty down the street just got a call last week saying her grandson was murdered. He was two years younger than Ray. I don't know what I would do if I got a call like that."

She put her hand on her heart. "I thank God every day that you and Mocha are safe at the dorm getting your education. I just wish Ray would have stayed and got his! He's a smart boy, too smart to be running the streets!"

I didn't speak; I couldn't. I felt too guilty and that was a feeling I was trying to avoid. I knew my actions would hurt her, and I didn't know if I was strong enough to handle that. Grandma Rae had always been there for me and given me everything I needed, and there I was planning to basically betray her. I felt like a snake in the grass, and I wanted to leave before I had to lie to her too. I finished the rest of the food on my plate and prepared to leave.

"How's school comin' along, honey?" Grandma Rae's voice was back to being soft and sweet.

Well, so much for not wanting to lie.

"Umm, it's OK," I answered. Not completely a lie.

I'm just planning on dropping out to start the biggest drug cartel Detroit has ever fuckin' seen, I confessed in my mind.

"That's good. Make sure you and Mocha are keeping them grades up," she said.

"Yes, ma'am." I grabbed my purse and stood to leave. "It was nice seeing you, Grandma Rae, I'm about to get back before Mocha think I got kidnapped."

"OK, honey, take this plate to that girl!" she handed me a heavy plate covered in foil. "And it was nice seeing you too. Oh, and if you see Ray, can you give him this?" She handed me a few envelopes that had Ray's name on them. "He keeps forgetting to take them. Call me to let me know you got home safe, you hear! And baby?"

"What's up, Grandma Rae?"

"You have a special heart," she started with her eyes staring into mine lovingly.

"And I'm going to do great things, Grandma, I know," I finished for her, smiling. She said that whenever she saw me. I gave her small frame a big hug and made my way to the front door. "Love you!" I called back to the kitchen before closing the door.

I walked quickly to my two-door coupe in the cold with the plate warm in my hands. I got in my car, set the plate on the passenger seat and began to eye the mail. I had the strongest urge to rip both envelopes open just to see a part of Ray's life I wouldn't see any other time.

Don't open it, Sadie, I told myself. *Don't. Open. It.*

After about one minute of a great debate in my head, I couldn't help myself. I ripped the first envelope open. What was inside made my eyes bulge. It was a bank statement that said Ray had just shy of half a million dollars in his account. I wasted no time in opening the second envelope. Inside that one was also a bank statement, that one with only two hundred thousand. Just as I was about to pull off en route to Uncle Rojer's auto shop, my phone began vibrating in my back pocket.

"Hello?" I said knowing it was Mocha calling without looking at the caller ID.

"Where are you at?" Mocha asked. "You never go anywhere without telling me."

"Damn, Mom, I didn't think you would be that worried," I said pulling off away from the curb in front of Grandma Rae's house.

"Shut up, bitch, after the mess you were talking, I thought you had gone out and done some stupid shit," she said.

She sounded as if she was seriously worried about me so I couldn't even be agitated.

"No, not yet anyways. I haven't talked to Ray yet. As a matter of fact, where are you at right now?" I asked.

"The dorm, obviously, bitch. How else would I know you aren't here?" I could hear her eyes rolling.

"Well, get in your car and meet me at Uncle Rojer's shop. You know Ray always helps out on Thursdays. I would rather talk to him about this face to face."

"OK," Mocha told me. "I'm leaving now."

"I'll see you there."

"Say?" she asked just as I was about to hang up the phone.

"What?"

"What if he says no? Then what?" she asked in all seriousness.

"Then nothing," I told her. "He's not going to say no."

"Well, look what the cat done dragged in!" Uncle Rojer greeted both Mocha and I when we walked into the garage. He and Ray were in the middle of working on a raggedy-looking green pickup truck when they heard our footsteps.

Ray turned around and smiled when he saw us.

"I was wondering when you two were going to come looking for me," he said wiping his hands off on a rag hanging from the pockets of his dirty overalls. "About a day late though."

For some reason, seeing Ray was different to me. For once, I didn't look at him as my big cousin who protected me and kept my pockets filled. I saw him as the street saw him. His presence demanded respect. He was the epitome of a boss, and I knew then that soon, Coopa's mistakes in the streets would get him caught up. I was at a loss for words with my cousin for a moment, but quickly, I regained my composure. He might've thought I was shook; but really, I was in awe.

"How are you doing, Unc?" I asked my uncle, not knowing what to say to Ray.

Uncle Rojer was a forty-four-year-old heavyset man, which was odd due to the fact that he was almost as tall as Ray.

"Tired!" Uncle Rojer's loud voice boomed. "Seems like every motherfucka in this city done broke their car!"

"It's what's bringing in your money, though, Unc," Ray chuckled.

"Yea, yea." Uncle Rojer began walking to the door leading to the inside of his shop. "Just make sure you lock up the place."

He waved bye to us. When I heard an engine start and the car drive off, I knew he was gone. I went and sat on a chair next to the truck that was previously being worked on.

"I have to go to the ladies' room." Mocha excused herself from the garage, and I knew what she was doing. "I'll be right back."

She shot me a look as she exited to the inside of the shop, and I knew she would be gone until things with Ray got squared away.

"So much for being ride or die," I said. I was hoping I would have her support in the matter of the conversation with Ray

"So, what's up, shorty?" Ray threw his towel to the side and pulled up a chair directly in front of me.

He knew what I wanted. He was testing me again. I wasn't going to let him intimidate me, especially with what I was asking for. What I wanted wasn't just given; it came at a cost. I had to prove that I was worth it.

"You know what's up, Ray. You've known since that day at the restaurant," I started. The way he was looking at me with those sharp eyes again I was almost unsure of myself. "Regardless if you help me or not, you know what lifestyle I want to live. The lifestyle I'm going to live. I'm not like my mom. You know the shit I dealt with coming up in Grandma Rae's house. Everybody knew about my momma being a hoe and was sure I would be just like that."

Ray's eyes stared intensely into mine; I could tell that he was latching onto every word escaping my mouth. He knew all of the stories about my mother. He probably knew some that even I didn't know, so I knew he understood what I was saying. But I needed him to *feel* what I was saying. I was only nineteen, but in my mind, I was double that.

"In some ways, I'm just like her. We're obviously attracted to the same things. But the difference is that I plan to be on top, never on the bottom. So what's up, boss? You gon' put me on or nah?"

I looked at Ray to see his exact reaction, but all I got was a look of sadness.

"Don't look at me like that," I said sternly to him. "Don't you fucking dare look at me like that!"

Ray sighed before finally nodding his head.

"OK . . . OK, it seems to me whether or not I help you, you're determined to make it into the game somehow. I would rather you be with me than against me. I know your drive. But just give me a minute, a'ight?"

"How long, Ray? When Coopa has your ass laid out in a ditch?" I asked him becoming upset that he was really trying to give me the runaround. "Real shit, Ray, the time is now or never."

I didn't like the fact that it seemed like Ray was Coopa's flunky, especially when Ray was the brains behind every operation. He was the reason Coopa's pockets stayed filled, and I didn't understand why Ray stood for it. Ray never had it in him to follow; he always had to be in the lead. But Coopa had a team and a connect, while Ray had only himself. So it seemed. If he was going to start, it was going to have to be from scratch, and I was willing to help build with him. Instead of responding to my words, however, Ray stood up and grabbed a duffle bag.

"I have to go get dressed. I'ma fuck with y'all later, OK?" he said, and with that, he left the garage.

I sat there dumbfounded, staring at the green truck. I couldn't believe he had just cut me off like that, like my conversation wasn't worth his time. I heard the door open to the shop once more, and I looked up to see Ray standing there staring at me.

"Keep your phone on OK, shorty?" he said smiling. "Something big is about to go down."

Before I could inquire on what the hell he was talking about, he was gone again. Seconds after his exit, Mocha reappeared. She saw the bewildered look on my face and held up her hands.

"What just happened?" she asked me, wanting to know all of the details.

"I-I don't know," I said honestly. "Come on, let's go." I stood up to leave the garage and ponder over Ray's words.

"Did you get your answer?" she pressed again walking after me.

"We'll see," I said and got into my car.

"I drove all the way down here for a fuckin' *we'll see*?"

"Yea," I told her. "You did. I'll see you back at home."

I started my car and sped off, leaving her on the sidewalk to inhale my exhaust. I knew that was rude since I'd told her to come meet me, but whatever. I had too many of my own thoughts to sort through. If Ray didn't accept my business proposition, I honestly didn't know what I was going to do with my life. I would rather be a broke homeless person on the street than stuck in a career I hated for the rest of my life. The streets were all I knew, and there was money in them. So why not invest? I couldn't help but to wonder what Ray was going to say when he called me; hopefully, something good.

Hopefully.

Chapter 7

Ray handed the shiny silver keys back to the owner of the green pickup and closed up the shop once it drove off. He was no longer in the dirty overalls that he wore on the days he chose to work at his uncle's shop. He'd gone to the bathroom in his uncle's office and taken a shower. When he emerged, he looked like a new man. Gone were the somewhat thuggish clothes he'd become accustomed to wearing. Replacing them was a light green Gucci button up that was slightly tucked into his tan Gucci slacks, and on his feet he wore light green Gucci dress shoes to match. The shoes added a nice touch, and with his dreads pulled back into a ponytail, Ray's appearance was very suave. As soon as he put on his coat and stepped out of the shop to lock the door, an all-black Mercedes with windows tinted so dark pulled up. You couldn't see who the passengers inside were. It slowed to a stop in front of the shop. Ray glanced down at the diamond-studded Rolex on his wrist gleaming back up at him. It read six o'clock.

Right on time, Ray thought to himself as he approached the vehicle.

Ray was supposed to be handling some business for Coopa. Word had it that another one of his houses had gotten hit. But if all went well, that wouldn't be Ray's problem any longer, so he didn't answer his call.

Lately, Coopa had been on some acting-funny shit with Ray, but Ray knew what was going on. He didn't speak about it, especially when people brought it to his attention, but he knew that Coopa was losing his grip on the game. Ray knew he'd been doing the thing that led to every great hustler's demise. He'd started smoking his own product. Ray had always been observant so he could tell by the slight twitch in Coopa's right eye and by the way he constantly rubbed his hands together that he was on drugs. Those were two things he didn't do before, and as soon as he started doing them, his empire began to crumble. Coopa also started to make poor choices in business and putting snakes on. He was putting his trust in all the wrong people. Within a year, almost half a million dollars came up unspoken for. No one knew that but Ray and Coopa, and that was another reason Ray didn't trust him. Coopa noticed all of that from the beginning but hadn't done anything to prevent it except kill the people he actually found out for sure were stealing from him. Why would Ray make an effort to save a man who couldn't save himself? The game was going to have its way with Coopa. Ray wasn't a fortune-teller, but he could see that.

Ray knew when he first started working with Coopa no good would come from it. His pockets would stay fat for a while, but he knew eventually the time would come when he would have to strike out on his own. Ray had the mind-set of a real man and the swagger of a hustler. He was intelligent, ruthless, and got every job done without a blemish. He knew that in order to set the operation off right, he would need a connect with some product that nobody had ever seen. It was backward a little bit because Ray had helped Coopa add on to his empire, only to take it into his own grasp. He knew Coopa wasn't going to bow without a fight. Ray had heavy artillery, but Coopa had heavy artillery and the manpower. For a while, Ray felt like an ant in the shadow of a shoe . . . until one night an unknown number hit his phone.

The voice on the other end of the phone belonged to one Ray had never heard before. Listening to the person speak, he knew it belonged to someone of Italian heritage. The person informed him that they'd been watching him very closely, and they liked the way he handled his business. Told him that they couldn't say much over the phone but to be ready at six p.m. the following Thursday in business attire.

"None of that thug shit."

Any other time, Ray would have been suspicious of a setup, but something in him told him it wasn't. He walked to the car, and the door opened for him. Ray entered the car with three Italians seated, all dressed in black Armani suits. Ray studied all of their hardened faces trying to read them, and, in turn, they did the same to him. To Ray's surprise, he recognized one of the men in the car as a man who'd been to his uncle's shop a few times for minor car problems. He'd told Uncle Rojer that he was just in town for a few days and wanted his vehicle inspected. His name was Vinny.

Vinny stared at Ray and was very impressed with his attire. He knew from the first day he met Ray that he was dealing with someone with potential. The way he knew numbers was impeccable. There would be no getting over on him. He could see by Ray's poise that he was different, unlike the two-bit street hustlers he'd grown accustomed to seeing in Detroit. The majority of them weren't about business, just quick cash, but with the information he'd dug up about Ray, he knew he would be the perfect attribute to his cartel. Vinny needed to expand his work. He didn't want to control any territory, he just wanted to get off his product. He was looking to be the supplier; however, he needed someone trustworthy and business savvy enough to supply to. At first he'd heard about a man named Coopa, but after scoping him out for a few days, he saw how sloppy he handled his work. Doing business with a man like him would be too much of a liability. Vinny needed someone he could depend on. Not someone who would end him up in federal prison.

After testing Coopa's product, Vinny knew for a fact that the hunger in Detroit was real because nobody wanted to deal with a plug who couldn't even deliver. Vinny heard about Ray through the grapevine and was pleased with what he'd seen. He had one of his men contact him and ready a meeting as soon as possible. The streets of Detroit were getting hungry, and Vinny had what their appetite craved.

"Gentlemen," Ray broke the silence nodding his head at the occupants of the Mercedes, and they returned the gesture.

"I believe we met indirectly before," Vinny said, holding his hand out from the far side of the backseat where he and Ray sat. "I am Vinny, and that's Eduardo," he nodded to the heavyset, slick-haired driver. "And that man right there is Stanley."

Stanley nodded at them from the passenger seat. His sleek black hair was combed up into a Mohawk, making his beaklike nose even more distinguishable. Stanley gave Ray the eye, and Ray stared back wondering why the muhfucka was staring at him. Stanley then nodded his approval to Vinny, who smiled wide. Vinny was a middle-aged man. He'd come from a wealthy family of mobsters, so he knew no other life than the dirty one he lived.

"This, my friends," Vinny pointed at Ray, "is the future! Ray, you're not new to this, so let us get straight into business."

"I couldn't have said it any better myself," Ray said cockily and got comfortable in his heated leather seat waiting for Vinny to continue.

"As I'm sure you know, Coopa has some very unhappy customers. He doesn't have what the streets are looking for, and pretty soon, he's going to pay for it. Probably with his life or his dick; one of the two." Vinny's accent was laying on thick with every word spoken. "The city needs some new work . . . and a new leader. Someone willing to get their hands dirty."

"So what are you proposing, Vinny?" Ray asked, cutting to the chase. "You got some work for me?"

Vinny chuckled at Ray's boldness, but little did he know Ray was just as deadly as him.

"You know how this shit works. To rule, you need a connect. I got what you're looking for," he told Ray, staring seriously into his eyes. "I'm not going to lie. I've been watching your every move for a few days now, and I like you, kid. You're smooth; the little operation you have going on is nice. I just don't know yet if I can trust you."

Ray nodded, agreeing with what he said. He didn't trust them either. He'd heard crazy things about the Italian cartel. They were up there with the Dominicans— definitely not anyone to be on any beef level with.

"However, I feel that you're the man who can get the job done. What I'm saying, Ray, is I need you," Vinny said. "None of that homo shit. This is strictly business. I need my work in Detroit, and I need you to push it."

Damn, these muhfuckas been following me? Ray thought to himself making a mental note to double security.

Ray sat taking everything Vinny was saying in, not trying to look too eager. But inside, he couldn't believe his luck.

"You want me to just be down with this proposition?" Ray asked. "I don't know you muhfuckas from a can of paint, so tell me what's really good?"

"I understand your caution, Ray. We randomly contacted you, and now we're offering you the place of a king. I can see where thoughts get skeptical, but I wouldn't even waste my time sitting here talking to you if this wasn't a serious business inquiry. I need a yes or no answer in thirty seconds, or I will take you back to your uncle's shop and we can pretend this conversation never happened . . . Well, until I send the choppers for you."

Damn, these muhfuckas really aren't playing around, Ray thought. *To be real they had me with that king shit.*

"A'ight, how much are we talking, and when are we doing this?" Ray asked.

"Smart man!" Vinny smiled, pleased with Ray's answer.

Eduardo and Stanley smirked at each other from the front seat, and Ray saw it, but he kept his cool. He knew he was playing ball in their field.

"I'm going to give you a little product first, just to see how fast you can get it off, and when you do, I'll give you more," Vinny explained.

Ray listened but wasn't with that plan at all. He already had a plan formulated, and he knew exactly what he was doing. Vinny was now just giving him a reason to go through with it instead of waiting.

"No, fuck that," he said shaking his head, surprising all of the passengers inside the vehicle. "If we're going to do this, we're doing it my way. My city, my rules. I'm a grown-ass man. Ain't no fucking way I'm about to just let you *give* me any product. Off tops, I'ma buy that shit and flip it in no time. Then I'll just re-up from there. I can't make a profit off another man's empire. Been there, done that. All I need from you is a team and artillery. I already have three ready to get it with me. I know once

Coopa catches wind on what's going on, it's going to be bloodshed. But honestly, right now, this money is more important."

Vinny sat taken aback but was beyond impressed on how the business meeting was being flipped around on him. Ray was definitely the right pick for the job.

"What are you saying, Ray?" Vinny asked him.

"What I'm saying is you need me as much as I need you. Otherwise, you would have never contacted me in the first place. Instead of putting yourself in some shit by fronting me, I'll just buy that shit and start my own operation. I'm not stupid or new to this, but you do need new blood, and that's me. I live and breathe the hustle, and I'll dead a muhfucka quick over my paper," Ray told him. "I'ma need to test your product first to see if it's even worth the hassle."

"Of course," Vinny nodded. "Stanley?"

On cue, Stanley handed Vinny a kilo of cocaine and a small pocketknife.

"Here you go." Vinny handed Ray the brick and sat back and watched, already knowing the value of his own product.

Ray made a small incision in the brick and tasted a small amount. He had been in the business long enough to use that as a method to level grades of cocaine, and Vinny's product had passed the test. He nodded his head in approval. He already saw the dollar signs flashing before his eyes, knowing he had the key to the city in his hands at that very moment.

"All right, coo, this is what I'ma have?" He had to make sure.

"Yes," Vinny informed him. "How many?"

"I'ma need thirty."

"Five hundred thousand," Vinny said instantly and watched to see if Ray would back down due to the price.

"Done." Ray didn't even flinch. "I'll give you a drop-off spot, and we'll make the exchange."

Vinny smiled one last time, knowing then that he'd made a longtime business partner. He reached out and shook Ray's hand again.

"All right, I'm going to set you up with this shit personally," Vinny said.

He liked how Ray conducted business. He was going to make his money regardless, and now he had a permanent buyer. Vinny was very pleased. They made plans to meet at a low-key spot Ray knew the next day.

"The shit here is garbage. People pay good money for the shit they smoke, inject, or snort. Why not give them their money's worth?" Vinny said to Ray as they pulled back in front of Uncle Rojer's shop. "Starting today, Ray, you are a king, not a street hustler. You're better than Coopa. Starting today, Detroit is yours. I have two people perfect for this . . . Don't worry, we did background checks on them, so loyalty is not a worry. You sure you can trust your people?"

"I'm one hundred percent sure," Ray told him, getting out of the car.

"All right . . . I'll see you soon, kid," Vinny said, and with that, he pulled off.

Ray pulled his cell phone out watching the black Mercedes round the corner and leave his sights. After phoning Sadie, Mocha, and Tyler informing them to meet him at his home, Ray decided to take a walk through his hood. He changed from suit and tie to a casual Diamond muscle shirt and a pair of cargo shorts. His bulletproof vest snug on his torso ensured that no bullet would penetrate, and the .45 on his hip dared a nigga to put his vest to use. He left his Escalade parked in the parking lot of the car shop and made his way on foot toward his Grandma Rae's house.

Putting his Wolf Grey 5s to use, he worked his way through the neighborhood he grew up in. Everything in it was a familiar sight. The houses were run-down; some yards cut and some weren't. Kids were running around like they didn't have any sense. Ray saw the swift moves of his young boys hitting the block. Fiends were everywhere begging for hits, but Ray didn't feed their hunger. None of the product they snorted could be tied back to him in any way. They were too messy. The last thing he needed was for one of them to get caught up with the law and start snitching. The people his boys served were high rollers who had an addiction to the candy Ray provided.

The feds had moved in and out of his block, even sent a couple of undercover cops to scope Ray's small operation. But when their bodies were found dismembered, that never happened again. Ray didn't move any product on his block, so any warrant to search it was deemed pointless. Out of all of the people Coopa put on, Ray's operation was the cleanest. Ray had a list of clients he served, and they bought in bulk, not by the hit. They always knew where one of Ray's workers would be posted on the block to place their order. A place and time would then be designated for a drop-off and pickup. First, of course, the money would have to be wired into an account that was opened and closed that same day. Ray had work moving all through Detroit, and he not only fed his block, but everyone else's too. He kept the block cleansed of Coopa's work. It was smart, but the real reason was out of respect for Grandma Rae.

People all around the way showed him love as he passed them. The daylight was completely gone, only to be replaced by streetlights. Ray saw the streets come alive. It was rare to see him walking anywhere, so many of the neighborhood rats tried to get his attention by swishing quickly in front of him or saying "Hi," flirtatiously. Ray only gave head nods and kept it moving while he tried to gather his thoughts.

As he walked and ignored the basic hoes cooing his name, he came across two of the most thorough youngins he had pushing for him. D and Amann were posted on a street corner engaged in a conversation with two young women. They were bad, and both had round bottoms, but when Ray was spotted, the two women were immediately dismissed. D and Amann were both in 501 Levis and retro Js. Their jewelry glistened with diamonds like the hood celebrities they were, and they both gave Ray a respectful smile.

"My mans!" D shook Ray's hand. "The fuck you doin' out here walkin', fam? We got Beamers and shit for all'at!"

Ray grinned because he was right. Bosses didn't walk, but in that instant, he needed the air to clear his mind, and a walk was what he needed.

"I'm chillin', fam," was Ray's simple response.

D and Amann were brothers. Not by blood, but it couldn't make them any closer. Through thick and thin, they had each other's back, and their loyalty in each other was what embedded Ray's trust in them. Out of every nigga Ray had working, the two of them put in the most work and brought home the most paper. They could hustle in their sleep, but the way they moved they never slept. At the age of twenty-two, they were also well tenured.

"What's been good, though?" Ray asked stopping to talk for a minute.

"Shit, shit," Amann answered. "Working."

"Yea, niggas been putting in overtime it seems, like just to fuckin' eat," D rubbed his hands together. "Upping prices."

"I see," Ray nodded, already knowing.

He knew all that was going on, especially after Coopa's trap was almost robbed. Coopa was messing up, and Ray had to pick up his slack. Unsatisfied clients made for angry workers, and that was bad for business. Everybody was just trying to eat, and that was something Ray understood. Coopa wasn't as in tune with the streets as he once was when he was living in them. He was selfish, and as long as his table was filled, he didn't care about anybody else's. Ray respected him because it was his work that had indeed put him on, but he also knew that once a person lost touch with the streets, there was no coming back from that.

"Aye, let me rap to you two about some shit real quick," Ray said making a decision then to put them on with his operations. D and Amann knew automatically by his tone that they needed to listen to what was about to be said. "You two niggas put in work. Loyalty is something that's hard to come by in this day and age. When you got it, you don't just throw it away. So I'd like to personally welcome you to The Last Kings. It's time to go to work."

Chapter 8

Words couldn't express my happiness when Ray called Mocha and I to meet him at his house to discuss a business opportunity. His beautiful five-bedroom home was ducked off in the suburbs of Detroit. He sat us down in his living room as soon as Tyler joined us. He then asked me how serious I was about taking my first steps into the game. He told us that he'd just come across a major move that he couldn't pass. Tyler was already down with the plan, and I was too. Mocha was the one who sat unsure. It made me a little agitated just because the idea of a drug cartel was her idea. The fact that she was trying to back out didn't sit right with me. What he was asking was dangerous I knew, but that was life. I knew how to hustle, how to break it down, and how to make my money quadruple. My life had been pledged to the game at an early age, and I was ready to carry out my destiny.

"You can't make people respect you," Ray told Mocha, and he pulled out two black boxes from underneath his long coffee table. "That's why you make them fear you. As long as you make your money and watch your back, it doesn't matter what anyone thinks of you."

He slid the boxes across the wooden table toward Mocha and me. Lifting the top of mine, my breath was short and sweet when I saw the inhabitants. Inside the box was a shiny .48-caliber pistol and two rounds sat next to it. I hesitated, but I picked it up and held it firmly in my hand. It felt natural.

"R-Ray, I don't know," Mocha said, staring at her handgun. "This is crazy."

"Yea, Ray," I had to agree with her. "You ready to go to war with Coopa?"

Ray nodded his head.

"The difference between Coopa and me is that I'm not going to have you two on any corner making drops. That's sloppy and out of date. This is going to be a business; I don't have time to be hot in these streets with the feds on my ass."

"What happened to loyalty, Ray?" Mocha asked him.

"Fuck that, Mocha," Tyler countered. "I've been tellin' my boy to strike out on his own for years now. Coopa don't know the first thing about being loyal, shorty."

"Right," I agreed with Tyler, eyeing my pistol. "Ray, if you got us, you know I'm down to ride for whatever."

"Say, I knew you would be down to ride," Ray smiled at me fondly. "What do you say, Mocha? How about we make this a family affair?"

"You say that shit like you're asking me to join a club or something! This is serious; we're talking about a drug cartel! As in a drug ring . . . as in some C. N. Phelps shit!"

"Phillips," I corrected.

"Yes, her! This is crazy, Say . . . crazy!" Mocha stared at her pistol.

"Mocha, what do you want to be in life?" I asked catching her off guard by the question.

"What? I don't know . . . Somebody who makes a lot of money. I don't know!"

"A boss?" Ray referenced.

"A boss," I concurred.

Mocha sighed and eyed all three of us before she finally nodded her head submissively.

"Yes, a boss."

"OK," I grabbed her hand. "Let's get this shit then; for the love of money, right?"

Our eyes met for a moment, seeming to connect us, making us one. Holding silent conversations was something Sadie and I did when we were younger, when she first came to stay with us. The words I spoke to her with my eyes were sincere. I was telling her that everything would be OK. Finally, Mocha blinked, breaking eye contact, and I knew she was in.

"OK, I don't even give a fuck!" She rolled her eyes. "I'm just worried about getting trigger-happy with this muhfucka!" Mocha aimed her pistol at Ray's white living-room wall and mouthed *"Pow."*

I laughed, happy that she finally was down with the program.

"Coo," Ray nodded his approval, eyeing everyone in the room. "We're a team now, so the only thing left to do is to make shit happen."

We did just that. Ray and Tyler already knew the rules of the game, and I was a little tenured in it as well. Ray took us under his wing, and in a matter of weeks, Mocha and I knew everything about the dope game a man could teach us.

"Everything else just comes with the territory," Ray told us.

Ray must have had some more change saved up from when he was working with Coopa because he went all out and bought a slew of Laundromats, an apartment complex, an Italian restaurant called Amore, a hair salon named Taste, and a strip club called Lace. Within months, Ray's work started spreading quickly like the flu bug through Detroit. No one knew who the carrier was, but everyone seemed to be feeling it. The team Ray set us up with was the truth. Besides the four of us, there were four other additions to our fam. They were obedient and ready to ride out whenever or wherever. When it came to distributing and collecting, they always delivered.

I'd become fond of the little Latina chick named Adrianna. She was a feisty little thing. She always pulled in double her weight and being in the big leagues didn't scare her. She was older than me by a few years, but she knew that I was the boss. She always made sure the money was counted right before it was delivered to Ray or me.

It was my idea to start a VIP club for our top wholesale clients. They were the only ones eligible to be members after a thorough background check. Ray thought the idea was brilliant and decided to add a kick to it. The buyers could test our product while getting pleasured. The spot was underground, literally, located in the basement of the Italian restaurant Ray had purchased, and if you didn't know it was there already, then you would never know.

Tyler came through with his connect with the feds. He broke him off a little paper here and there to be kept informed on the moves of the police. That way, we would always have some type of heads-up. After that, it was a wrap. It was clear that we were slowly but surely taking the city over, and it was a beautiful thing. Ray had stopped all involvement with Coopa completely, and I knew that wasn't going to end well, but I trusted his judgment. Coopa wasn't the only one anymore with a team of riders. If anything popped off, there would definitely be a war scene in the streets of Detroit. Ray made sure that Mocha and I were never alone wherever we went and told us to always stay strapped.

"Niggas hate seeing a come up," he kept saying, and I knew he was referring to Coopa.

After Mocha and I dropped out of school, we began living with Ray in his home since it was big enough. Five rooms, four bedrooms, two kitchens, a theatre in the basement, and Ray even had the audacity to have a fountain in his entryway. Those were just some of the highlights. Ray had really outdone himself with his house, and I was proud that he'd come that far. One night when just he and I were home, I brought it to his attention while we counted stacks of money to maybe let Coopa in on the action, keep the love in the city. I didn't see the point in going to war in your own hometown. The money would bè doubled and be kept flowing. It made sense to me. However, Ray disagreed.

"Nah, Say. Coopa isn't the type to just shake hands and step down from the throne. Detroit is his in his eyes. Unless somebody knocks him down from his seat, he ain't going nowhere," he said putting me on game.

"So, what are we going to do when he jumps?" I asked him. "'Cause you know that nigga is going to jump."

"You know what's going to happen, Say." Ray touched the steel he kept on his waist. "That nigga is either going to bow down or lay down. My city ain't going down just because a boss can't stay a boss. Fuck that. It's all about this here."

He grabbed a stack of hundreds and waved them in the air.

"A nigga will do crazy things for this, Sadie. Just remember not to be that crazy," Ray told me and sighed. "Coopa is going to try to stop this. I'm on the rise, and his position as kingpin is being threatened. But I know him; he's not going to come for me directly. I know his style. He's going to come for what I hold dearest to my heart. You and Grandma Rae."

What Ray was telling me made sense. I then understood the reason why he made Mocha and me stroll the city with five soldiers each.

"I got niggas at her house around the clock," Ray informed me, seeing the worry on my face.

"She's OK with that?" I asked, astounded knowing Grandma Rae hated random muhfuckas in her home.

Ray grinned at me through the freshly twisted dreadlocks dangling freely in front of his face.

"Hell nah, Say. You know she would flip if she knew them niggas were there!"

I grinned too, but then became serious again.

"Ray, I just want you to know I can handle myself," I told my cousin. It was rare when I got him to myself, and I wanted to reassure him that letting me into his cartel wasn't a bad idea. "This is nothing to me. I'm not scared of a fuckin' Coopa or any nigga who might come for me. If you got me, I got you, remember?"

Ray smiled and nodded his head.

"I feel you, Say, and I know you can handle yourself. I'ma just make it so you never have to." He stood up and started dumping the money in bags, preparing to make a drop to re-up. "Where's Mocha?"

I shrugged my shoulders. "She made a trip to visit a friend in Atlanta. She'll be back in a few days," I told him, not letting it show on my face that I missed my best friend.

I knew Mocha was from Atlanta, so I didn't mind her taking a few trips to her hometown. It was rare when we weren't together, especially since we both dropped out of school to tend to business. I knew I wasn't going to be anybody's executive but the dope man's, so I didn't want to waste any more of my time. Ray was upset with the decision, but we stood firm by it.

"You been coo?" Ray studied me where he stood.

"Yea, I've just been kicking it hard with Adrianna. That's my bitch. She's a fucking thug, dude," I said, thinking fondly of my new friend.

"Yea, she's ride or die. I had to have her in on this shit. Loyalty is all I need. When Mocha gets back, we're havin' a meeting. There's some other shit I need to bring to the table. It's been a few months now, and the money is rolling in. I need to know where all y'all muhfuckas' heads are at, you feel me?"

"All right, I'ma hit that bitch up and tell her to get her ass home ASAP," I told him and pulled out my cell phone.

Chapter 9

Ray set up a meeting with everyone as soon as Mocha got back in the city. We sat eight deep around the large table in his dining room. All but two of the chairs were filled, and everybody who was supposed to be there was in attendance. It was a still night in Detroit. The weather had finally begun to warm as we said good-bye to the winter season. The moon shone in on us all through the glass patio door beside the table. Tyler sat on Ray's right side, while I sat on the left. Mocha sat beside me, and Adrianna beside her. Devynn was a young, beautiful woman with smooth chocolate skin and long, soft, natural curls sitting atop of her head. She packed two chrome pistols on each thigh and getting on her bad side would get two clips a home inside your skull. I honestly thought I would have a problem with her, but surprisingly, she proved me wrong.

Next to her sat D, short for Deion. He was big and swole, and he didn't need his burner to rock anyone to sleep. His fists were lethal weapons themselves. His Jamaican heritage gave him a very distinct look. His dreads were short and thick, and his eyes were too close together, but he knew how to hustle and aim a gun, so he was good for the team. He was good people, and his loyalty to Ray spoke volumes.

Last but not least was Amann. He had a smooth baby face but harbored a ruthless mentality. Since his girlfriend and two-year-old daughter were killed in the cross fire of a robbery, he thought with the 9-mm pistol that he had strapped to his waist. He'd lost everything, so spilling blood was like kicking over a bucket of water to him. Amann was someone a person would send in to get the job done. His heart was buried with the body of his baby girl. The only things he believed in were loyalty and getting money. Anybody who got between him and that would surely get put to rest. I was in a room full of cold-blooded killers, the type of people who put bullets in folks like shots from the doctor, and I had never felt more at home.

Ray stood up from where he sat at the head of the table and eyed each and every person around him, even Tyler.

"Hello, ladies and gentlemen," he started with a smirk. "If you're wondering why you're here, then you need to get up and out of my fuckin' house."

No one moved; everyone knew what was up, and Ray nodded his head.

"That must mean you know why you're here. You know who you are." Ray started to walk slowly around the rectangular table. We all glanced around, becoming familiar with each other's faces.

We all knew of each other, but it was the first time we'd all been together in one room. We all had been doing our solo thing and getting off the product Ray purchased from his mysterious connect in time to re-up. I nodded my head at everyone around the table in greeting.

"This," Ray raised his hands motioning to everyone at the table, "is the team. The goal is to get this dirty money quick and flip it even faster. I would also like to say congratulations. You've proved to me that you all are about your paper, and it was you who built the foundation of this operation. I'm impressed . . . I've never seen a team of only eight people flip work so fast. The profit I made off those bricks was more than even I expected. We're taking over the game. This is the beginning of a new wave.

I nodded my head, feeling empowered by Ray's words.

"I grew up in these streets watching the hustlers before me slang dope on the corners. Watching their come up and because of their flashiness and cockiness, I saw their demise too. That's not going to be us . . . Kings live forever! *This?*" Ray pointed his two pointer fingers toward the ground. "This is the whole operation, here in this room. If I eat, we all eat. Period."

The room remained silent, and I appreciated the respect they all had for Ray. He stood over us as a leader . . . the head of The Last Kings. It was his time, and I think everyone at that table knew it.

Fuck Coopa, I thought.

My allegiance lay with Ray. We were his soldiers, his shooters, and the people who would stand by his side. We could be out in the murderous streets of Detroit slanging tiny bags of coke to the neighborhood crack-heads doing anything to support their habit; instead, we were a part of something much bigger. The name "Last Kings," fit perfectly as I stared at everyone around the table. There was something that we all had in common; we were all orphans. Sadly, we were all each other had, no matter how short of a time we'd known each other.

"All these businesses I'm running are cleaning this dirty money, so I don't ever want to see any of you moving on the streets." Ray's voice held not a hint of humor, letting us all know he was serious. "That's the old way of the hustle, and moving that way could jeopardize this whole operation. If I find any of you doing that, I will dead you where you stand, no matter who you are. Also, Coopa is expecting that shit. None of my soldiers are going to get caught slipping. So I'm about to put it to you all like this . . ."

Ray went back to his seat at the head of the table, and upon sitting down, he reached under the table and pulled out seven folders. I felt Mocha lean in slightly, and I saw the anticipation on her face.

"Seven kings around me and six businesses. It's been two months, and like I said, each of you have proven to me that you can pull in your own work. Now, it's time for some *real* work. Each of you will manage one of my businesses."

My mind began reeling. Ray was a genius. The cartel would be run behind our businesses, meaning there would be no dirty money. The first two months of our hustle had been building up our clientele, and thanks to my idea for the club, all of their names were listed. As long as we could deliver, they weren't going anywhere. Ray's connect had the best product around town, and it was going to make us rich. I couldn't help the grin that formed on my face. I wondered how long Ray had been planning it, because what he had pitched was flawless.

"My man Ty here has the fed activities in check, so if he calls, you better answer your phones on the first ring. No questions asked. Sadie?" Ray turned his attention to me.

"Yes?" I inquired taking a sip of the champagne before me.

"Amore is yours," he told me, and I was slightly taken aback.

Everyone sitting at the table stared at me. We all knew that not only was Amore the Italian restaurant Ray owned, but it was the heart of the whole operation. I thought that he would make Tyler the head of it, and by the expression on Tyler's face, I knew our minds were thinking the same thing. Our eyes met for a moment before I averted them back to Ray.

"Ray, are you sure about that?" Tyler asked him skeptically.

It kind of set me off slightly, like he didn't think I could do it or something.

"You forget she's the reason *why* the restaurant is a big part of this whole deal," Ray told Tyler while smiling confidently at me. "I'm positive, and plus, she'll have Mocha right there beside her making sure that everything is running smoothly."

Tyler backed off, but I could tell he wasn't very happy with Ray's decision. I, on the other hand, felt honored that Ray had put me in such a position of power. It proved that he had trust in me beyond measure and my respect for him rose. He then continued on to appoint everyone else their station. Tyler would head the chain of Laundromats, Devynn was put head of the hair salon, D was set up to be the landlord of the apartment buildings, Adrianna would manage the nightclub Lace, and Amann was entrusted with the convenience store Ray had recently purchased. Ray slid a folder in front of each of us. I opened mine and noticed that it contained the blueprints of Amore with several escape routes.

"You will all learn the blueprints of the buildings. A boss is never caught slipping in his own place of business. There are undetectable stash spots in every building. Learn them. There are also artillery rooms in every building. Keep them stocked," Ray told us. "This is the last movement Detroit will ever see."

"The Last Kings," I said and raised my glass feeling that it was the right time to do so.

"The Last Kings!" they all said in unison and raised their glasses as well.

Before we could drink our toast, I noticed a red dot slowly moving to the center of Mocha's forehead. Instinct set in, and I pushed her out of her chair. No sooner had she hit the floor did the glass patio door shatter and a bullet hit the wall behind where she had been sitting. After that first bullet, it seemed as though hundreds more followed. Everyone was caught off guard as we saw at least fifteen hooded masked figures in all-black appear in the backyard shooting rogue bullets into Ray's home.

"Get down!" Tyler yelled, and we all ducked trying to dodge bullets.

Devynn and Adrianna pulled out their burners in a matter of seconds and began shooting expertly at the advancing enemy. I watched as their bullets caught their marks, making the victims' heads snap back before pulling out my own pistol. Before I could get my first shot off, Ray grabbed my arm, preventing me from standing to my feet.

"Get to the garage!" Ray ordered Mocha and me as he popped two of the men trying to get through the patio door.

I snatched my arm from him.

"Fuck that!" I stared at Mocha who was frozen on the ground in shock and fear, not knowing what to do. "It's OK," I whispered to her.

Just as the words left my mouth I heard noise coming from the living room and looked up in time to see a hooded figure aiming for our two bodies on the ground. I quickly pointed my gun at him and put two neat holes in his dome, making his body fall back into the three coming up from behind him. It gave Mocha and me time to stand to our feet and squeeze our triggers, killing them where they stood. What was supposed to be a simple business meeting had turned into a battlefield. There were bullets whizzing past my head left and right. God must have had my back because I didn't even feel a graze. In their case, strength didn't come in numbers because they were fighting a losing battle. They were sloppy, and it was obvious with their bodies piling that they hadn't thought their plan all the way through.

"You wanna play, huh? You wanna play, bitch!" I heard Adrianna's rants as she clicked heartlessly on the intruders.

"These muhfuckas is sad, yo!" Devynn actually laughed as she put five bullets in one body and reloaded taking cover behind Adrianna.

From out of nowhere, I heard the sound of automatic rounds being let out, and I knew for sure that we were all goners. It wasn't until I saw D and Amann toting AK-47s and finishing off the remainder of the intruders that I relaxed. Finally, the blazing stopped, and all of our guns were smoking. Ray's house, which was usually neat and tidy, was totally destroyed and bloody. The body count of the dead totaled up to at least twenty. There was a slight groan in the air, and all of our attention averted to the ground. One of the intruders was still moving and trying to crawl away. He was closest to me so I walked up behind him placing my foot on his back. He grunted at the pain from the weight of my foot and the bullets wedged in his body caused blood to spill from the wounds. Bending down, I snatched the mask from his face and instantly recognized him as Antwan, Mocha's old boo. I looked back at Ray, who smiled and shook his head.

"Your mans sent you to my home to dead me?" Ray walked up to him and kicked him in his face so hard I saw a few teeth slide along the stained red carpet. "I would have you give that nigga a message for me . . . but your body in a duffle bag should do just fine."

Ray raised his gun slightly and put a bullet in each of Antwan's eye sockets.

"Bitch nigga," Ray spat. "We have to move. I know the neighbors heard all that shit. I also know that if none of his men return to tell him that the job he sent them on is done, he's going to send another sweep in. Get a cleaner team here in two point five, Tyler. Adrianna, take Mocha and Sadie somewhere to lay their heads for the night. The rest of you know what to do. Hit the block, find this nigga. This nigga sent these pussies to my house? It's war."

Ray was barking orders before it registered in anyone's head what had just happened. His gangster shone as he was never knocked off his A-game, no matter the situation.

"I'm not leaving you," I told my cousin, worried about him.

Ray had been wrong; he thought Coopa wouldn't try him. The scene there proved that Coopa was taking Ray's come up to the heart and wanted him out of the game—bad. So bad that he hadn't even thought thoroughly about his plan of action. All his shooters lay dead, their souls floating above us. If Coopa was that clouded by anger, there was no telling what his next malicious act would be. I refused to leave my cousin's side.

"Sadie, this isn't something to negotiate," Ray told me his voice slightly soft. He knew I was worried, and he hugged me, handing Adrianna a wad of hundreds. "Take my bulletproof Hummer and park it somewhere low. I'll call you in the morning."

Adrianna nodded her head, knowing that protecting Mocha and I was her job.

"Let's go," she instructed a little forcefully and grabbed us by the arms.

"Ray!" I called back at him, not able to break away from Adrianna's tight grip on my arm.

"I'll call in the morning," Ray promised again.

"Sadie, it's going to be OK; for now, we need to listen to Ray," Mocha told me.

I obliged, and with one last look at my cousin's enraged face, I followed Adrianna to refuge and out of harm's way

Chapter 10

It seemed to Ray that Coopa was suddenly an invisible man. After the fiasco at Ray's home, Coopa had doubled up on his protection. He had decoys for days and stayed at least twenty deep wherever he went. Coopa was playing it safe, especially after the bodies of the dead were delivered packed in boxes at his front door. He knew that Ray was not someone to take lightly. Something he honestly should have known from working with him for years. Coopa had watched Ray's rise but hadn't paid enough attention to it because out of all of Coopa's goons, Ray had always been the least flashy. Ray didn't have a slew of women or baby mamas, nor was he tricking off. Coopa knew then, when it was too late, that he should have wondered what Ray was doing with all of his money. Stacking up was what he had been doing, and when Coopa caught wind of an underground movement happening in his city, he flipped. He was even more enraged when he learned through the street vine that Ray was the head of the whole operation. When he sent his goons to move in on Ray, he had underestimated the strength of Ray's little army. He thought for sure they would be killed in the ambush, and he would just go back to running Detroit with an iron fist the next day. How wrong had he been . . . None of his men made it home to their families, and he was to blame for that. But that was the least of his worries; he only cared about his own well-being. He'd seen firsthand how Ray got down. His aim was flawless. It was the reason he wanted him on his team in the first place. Coopa knew that with a killer like Ray, he needed the extra protection, and being caught slipping would most definitely cost him his life.

He stayed low, sending his most loyal men to handle his business. There was a big drop coming up, and he knew that his empire couldn't risk the loss of the possible new connect. JoJo, Coopa's new right-hand man, was sent in Coopa's place to the Italian restaurant Amore and was expected to conduct business on Coopa's behalf. Coopa heard that some big-time Italian man had some fantastic product. He knew if he got that in his streets, he would have what they had been crying for. Coopa wasn't stupid; he could see his streets getting hungry. At first, he didn't care as long as he was still on top. But it didn't take long for niggas to turn and think they would get away with hitting licks on his trap houses. Coopa had to turn things around because he would rather drink piss than kneel at the feet of a man *he* put on.

Ray wanted to move on Coopa but refused to let anger cloud his judgment. He knew Coopa wasn't going to be stupid enough to come directly at him again, so he felt comfortable in his position. Business would have to continue; The Last Kings were only at the beginning of their rise. Ray sat in the back of Amore, awaiting the arrival of a new potential client.

Although Vinny was just the connect, he felt a strange draw to Ray. He had been in the world of cocaine all of his life, and it was rare to see things change for the better. He knew from the first day of speaking to Ray that he would bring something to the game that had never been done before. Ray and Vinny spoke often, and he played his best hand in Ray's business. He wanted Ray's operation to succeed. When Ray told him about everything that was going on, he could have easily taken Coopa out of the game; one hit. But he knew that this was something Ray must do on his own to earn his rite of passage to the throne. He knew Ray's eyes were on the prize: Detroit. He also knew that Coopa knew the city like the back of his hand. Meaning, touching him would be almost impossible . . . almost. Since Vinny touched down in Detroit, Coopa had been trying to make contact, but Vinny didn't want to give him his business. He felt he was too incompetent and foolish to push his work. Vinny made a phone call and set the meeting up, knowing that no one in the city knew about Ray and his connection. He rolled the dice; it was up to Ray to determine what they landed on.

A man wearing Ralph Lauren cargo shorts and a blue Ralph Lauren Polo entered Amore. Although he wore sunglasses to shield his eyes, Ray recognized him as a man he had put in a lot of work with. JoJo glanced around the restaurant trying to spot his contact, and Ray quickly stood up as a tall waiter passed, walking at his pace to shield his body. Once he made it into the large kitchen, he walked quickly to the secret entrance of the club. He thought quickly. JoJo was there to conduct business, which meant Coopa clearly couldn't have known that Ray was the contact. Ray couldn't let JoJo see him; he had to find a new connect. Sadie and Mocha were automatically out of the equation. Everyone knew their connection with Ray. Plus, he had them handling a major deal at that time. D and Amann were out making a few drops, and Devynn just didn't fit the role. When Ray stepped foot in the dimmed lighting of the club, he walked the long hallway in search for Adrianna. He had to find her quickly, before JoJo thought it was a setup and left. Ray passed several rooms. Each had a valuable customer testing his product to ecstasy.

He found Adrianna in the Money Room counting and bagging. When she saw Ray, she smiled very sexily up at him. Her smile was flawless, and she wet her lips with her tongue. She wore her long silky brunette hair in a ponytail, and her attraction to him read easily on her face, but her actions spoke another story. She was a woman scorned, and she didn't want to get involved emotionally with another hustler. She knew it wasn't forever. After being the ride-or-die chick for two big-time hustlers and watching one get tortured and killed and the other's brains blown out, she decided that she would only be in the game to make her money, not for love. However, being in Ray's presence proved to be difficult. He was different than any other man she'd ever encountered.

The rising attraction Adrianna felt for Ray was definitely mutual. Ray was attracted to her ruthless swagger. She wasn't afraid to die, nor was she afraid to kill an enemy. She was the type of woman who rode shotgun, with a shotgun. Ray saw more than the image she tried to spit out for others to see; he saw way deeper than that. He read her pain easily only because she hid it so well. Adrianna was really just a soft bluff. The way Adrianna looked at him, Ray knew it was best not to get involved. It was clear that he already had one soft spot, Sadie, and mixing business with pleasure was never a good thing. He knew that if he allowed himself to get too close to Adrianna, he would get too attached, and love got you killed, and in Adrianna's case, she knew that too well. For now, Ray knew that business was all that could be between them.

"I need you," Ray started and instantly saw Adrianna's face change. "Chill, ma," Ray said not wanting to give her the wrong idea. "Business as usual."

Her face dropped, and she rolled her eyes. She wasn't going to lie; she was disappointed. It was random of Ray to just pop up on her and a little piece of her was hoping he wanted to lay her down on the counting table and have his way with her.

"What's up, *boss?*" she asked, putting extra emphasis on her last word in sarcasm.

She didn't mind Ray keeping her at a respectable distance. It made her urges easier to keep under control. The old Adrianna would have gotten at Ray quickly and easily, but she had left the "wifey" life behind. Ray briefed her on the situation, and before he even finished telling her the plan, she was down to ride.

"A'ight," Adrianna nodded her head, her New York accent thick. She threw the remaining money stacks into a duffle bag and stood up. "Dude is upstairs now?"

Ray nodded his head.

"Yea, ma." He looked her up and down determining then that what she was wearing was sexy enough to entice JoJo's tiny brain.

Adrianna was looking quite edible wearing a Gucci hoodie with red embroidery that fit snugly on her upper half. The Levi jeggings she wore hugged her wide hips just right, and Ray couldn't help but to notice how beautiful she was. Her almond-colored skin seemed to glow. She wore her hair pulled back, allowing her high cheekbones and bright round hazel eyes to be very distinguishable. With her full lips and plump breasts, she was what most would call a bad bitch.

"Aye, ma, you got this hard chick act goin' on. I need you to sexy it up a little for me," Ray instructed. "Take them sneakers off; Mocha has a pair of Christians in that cabinet over there. Put them on and let's go to work."

Adrianna nodded her head, pleased with the look of lust she saw in Ray's eyes. It was only there for a split second as he eyed her body, but she caught it.

"Don't worry, papi, I got this," she said sincerely, putting the pumps on her feet.

She pulled the ponytail holder out of her hair, letting it fall in soft curls around her face. Winking at Ray, she led the way to the restaurant. Her job was simple: flirt with JoJo, make a deal, and then get him to come home with her . . . Well, to a hotel room that evening. Ray knew JoJo was his key to Coopa, and he couldn't fuck it up. With JoJo's long list of baby mamas, Ray knew that all he needed was a little liquor in his system for him to take the bait.

"Don't fuck up, ma," he said briefly, grabbing her arm.

Adrianna paused before stepping through the secret door that led into the kitchen of the restaurant.

"Like I said, I got this." She gently removed her arm from his grip and smirked with a wink. "Oh . . . Don't get jealous, baby."

Ray smiled as he watched her sashay away. He didn't doubt her for a moment.

Adrianna walked seductively to the king-sized bed inside of the bedroom in the hotel suite. The lights were dimmed, and Trey Songz was playing softly in the background. All it took were a few shots of Hennessey in his system, and he was ready to jump her bones.

This is who Coopa has workin' his fuckin' team? Fuckin' pathetic! Adrianna thought disgustedly, while smiling at JoJo who lay naked on the bed.

She wore a sexy red bra and thong set and with every little movement, her ass jiggled. She was used to men going crazy over her frame and her smooth almond skin, so the hungry expression on JoJo's face was nothing new to her. She wanted to laugh. One, because he was ugly as fuck and black, and two, because she wondered exactly what the fuck he thought he was going to do with his tiny five-inch penis. Dancing seductively toward him, she turned around and began making her round ass cheeks clap.

"You want me, daddy?" she whispered.

JoJo's eyes were glued to the two saucers before them; all he could do was nod his answer.

"Good," she licked her lips and proceeded to crawl up the bed until she was directly over him. "How do you want me?"

"Just like this, baby." JoJo gripped both of her cheeks tightly, one in each hand.

Adrianna giggled and positioned herself over him. She began teasing him by grinding on his hardness, letting him feel her wetness. JoJo threw his head back in pleasure.

"Damn, ma! I can't wait to dive into this shit. Fuck!"

Adrianna laughed, knowing he would never dive into anything ever again except a grave. She placed her hands on his and removed them from her cheeks, and then slid them up the bed above his head. Her body was positioned in an arc, with her knees on the side of his hips. She looked into his thirsty eyes and smiled slyly before yelling . . .

"Now!"

On cue, Ray entered the hotel room with the key Adrianna had snuck to him when JoJo made a dash to the restroom.

"What the fuck?" JoJo exclaimed, seeing the raised gun pointing at him.

"What up, JoJo?" Ray smirked at the naked man before him.

He walked over to where Adrianna had undressed JoJo. Taking notice of how luscious Adrianna looked in her lingerie, he kicked JoJo's clothes to the side.

"You have thirty seconds to tell me where Coopa is." Ray cocked his gun, allowing Adrianna time to climb off of the bed.

"Ray, man—" before JoJo could get the words out of his mouth, he had a bullet in his leg.

"Twenty seconds," Ray said as blood spilled all over the bed from JoJo's oozing leg.

"Ray, please," JoJo said in pain, seeing his life flash before his eyes. "I don't know where that nigga is!"

Ray shot his gun again. The silencer made a soft *"pft"* as a bullet caught JoJo in his torso.

"Ten seconds," Ray said coldly, aiming his gun at the thing JoJo definitely didn't want to lose. He wasn't there to talk or to listen to a begging-ass nigga.

"Ahh!" JoJo breathed heavily, trying to cradle his wounds. That didn't stop him from talking shit, though. "Fuck you, nigga! You ain't shit but what Coopa made you—*nothing*. I ain't no snake-ass nigga like you, pussy! You're trying to take something that ain't yours, nigga. Did you think war wasn't going to break out? Coopa is going to dead ya ass, bruh."

Ray laughed at JoJo's words, knowing that he was just a dead man talking. He wanted to see how much about his words JoJo really was. Ray cocked his gun and shot a bullet real close to JoJo's penis, although he made sure he didn't hit it . . . this time. JoJo let out a scream so loud Ray would have sworn a little girl was somewhere hiding in the room and just like the chicken Ray knew he was, he began clucking out information.

"That nigga said he had business to attend to. You may actually know about it," JoJo was breathing rigidly but still managed to let out a sick smile. "*Morgan Towers* ring a bell?"

A red flag went up in Ray's head, and Adrianna looked at him, already knowing what was wrong. Morgan Towers was where Mocha and Sadie had set out to make a deal with one of their usual customers. It was a run-down apartment building. He rented out an apartment there to do some of his major deals. It was a perfect spot just because it was so obvious, and he'd been using it for years. He'd been using it for so long, he should have known that Coopa would have caught wind at what exactly took place there. JoJo began laughing controllably.

"You can kill me now," he said, blood trickling down the side of his mouth. "But your cousin will be joining me soon."

He still had a smile on his face when Ray lit his body up with the rest of his clip.

"Bitch," he spat on his dead body.

"Ray, we have to go!" Adrianna said already fully dressed. She grabbed her clutch purse and ran for the door.

Ray began trying to get ahold of Sadie by calling her cell phone, but it just went straight to voice mail. Same with Mocha.

"Fuck!" Ray exclaimed as they ran through the hotel trying to make it to the exit.

Adrianna saw the worry all over Ray's face. She couldn't lie and say she wasn't worried too. If Coopa had gone himself to where Sadie and Mocha were to make a drop, nothing good could come out of it. Coopa was a weak leader, but she knew how merciless of a killer he was. She also knew that Sadie and Mocha were inexperienced when it came to the murder game. She hoped that they wouldn't become victims.

Please let us get there in time, Adrianna said a silent prayer, hopping into Ray's Escalade. They hit eighty across town, knowing that two of their peoples' lives were on a countdown.

Chapter 11

Mocha and I entered the apartment with the key Ray had given me. Larry, the guy Ray had sent us to meet, was supposed to be in the living room waiting for us. It was supposed to be a simple pickup, not more than five minutes. But as soon as I stepped foot in the two-bedroom apartment, I knew that walking back out might not have been an option that we had. Mocha inhaled sharply when she saw Larry's body lying facedown on the carpeted floor, a pool of blood formed neatly around his head.

"Sadie—" Mocha started but never finished.

Four men made their presence known walking from the back rooms. They all had their guns drawn. My heart stopped when I recognized one of the men as none other than Coopa. My mind wrapped around what the fuck was happening. Coopa had to have set us up, and I felt my heart twist into knots. He stared coldly at the two of us standing there.

"Some bitches?" He eyed us up and down and laughed. "This is how Ray conducts his business?"

Coopa was a good-looking light-skinned older man, but the way his face was always turned up took the handsome out of his appearance. He kept his head cut bald, probably because he was balding up top, and the goatee on his face was neatly trimmed. He stood before us at six foot two in a tan Armani suit with the matching shoes. Coopa motioned for his men to check us, which they did gladly, removing every weapon we had on our bodies, but they left my clutch in my hands. When they were done, Coopa began to pace slowly in front of us.

"I heard through the grapevine that there was a new operation starting in Detroit, and I thought, 'Nah, not my city!' Don't no work come through this muhfucka if I don't know about it! Imagine my shock when I found out Ray was the snake goin' under my nose trying to take what's mine!" He waved his hands to the duffle bags of money on the couch that contained the two hundred and fifty thousand we were there to pick up. "Look at this shit! Two hundred and fifty stacks I would have been missing out on . . . Do you see the error in this fuckin' equation? That's *my* fuckin' money! *Mine!*"

Coopa stopped pacing to stand directly in front of me and looked into my eyes. He grabbed my face and, squeezing hard, pulled it close to his. At that moment, seeing the lust in his eyes, I regretted wearing my skinny Miss Me jeans with only a green tank top. The weather was nice. I didn't expect to have to dress to get robbed. I smelled his scent and knew that too had to be an Armani fragrance, hating how nice it was. I tried to turn away. I caught a glimpse of Mocha and admired the hardened look she had on her face. I knew she was terrified, and I immediately was consumed with guilt knowing it was my fault she was in that predicament in the first place. She looked back at me and gave me a look that said everything would be OK, like she knew exactly what I was thinking. Her head was held high as the men around her tried to spook her with their guns.

They'd gotten me for all of my weapons . . . except for one. I had a .22 Magnum revolver in my clutch loaded and ready to bust at the right moment. Coopa surprised me by grabbing my ass harder than anyone ever had.

"Don't fucking touch me," I glared at him, trying to push him away from me.

I didn't give a fuck about the guns pointed my way anymore. I didn't like the way Coopa was licking his lips at me. Flashbacks of Nino began popping up in my head, and I wanted nothing more but for them all to be erased.

"Bitch!" Coopa snatched me up by my neck so fast I barely had time to take a breath. "You working for this nigga who's stealing from me *and* you his family. You're about to pay a small part of his debt to me!"

Mocha dashed over to where Coopa had me and jumped on his back, beating him with her fists.

"Get the fuck off of her!" she screamed and bit his ear like Mike Tyson.

Coopa yelled in pain before he got control and flung her off of his back.

"Get that bitch!" he directed his henchmen. "One of y'all should have shot her!"

One of the men, a fat, dark-skinned man who probably got no pussy, grabbed for Mocha, but she swung and connected with his jaw. The slap he landed on her face was so brutal the sound echoed throughout the apartment.

"Mocha!" I screamed, trying to push Coopa off of me.

I saw blood trickling down her nose and wanted to get over to where she was. Coopa laughed at my feeble attempts, knowing I couldn't overpower him. He picked me up and carried me to one of the bedrooms in the back. No matter how much I kicked or screamed, I couldn't get free. He tossed me on the bed in the master bedroom like a pillow and locked the door behind him. I wanted to cry, hearing Mocha's desperate screams of my name over and over.

"No point in trying to run, ma." Coopa grabbed my Fendi clutch and threw it to the side of the bed.

The soft thud it made was slightly noticeable, but Coopa paid it no mind. He was too busy forcing my pants off. I spat on him.

"I'm going to kill you," I snarled in an icy tone.

I sounded so confident that he fumbled with my pants a bit. He regained his composure quickly, however, as he pulled a handkerchief from the pocket of his suit jacket. I knew that Coopa, like Nino years before, was going to take something that I would never willingly give to him. Chuckling, Coopa threw the handkerchief to the side and gave me his pearly white smile.

"Feisty! And you got a fat ass," he winked at me. "This should be fun."

Coopa then removed his pants and jacket. In those few moments, I made the decision to not fight it. Every odd was against me, and my goal was to get to my clutch. The prize lay inside it. Coopa was slipping by letting me stay alive longer than necessary to get his self-proclaimed money. I closed my eyes and tried not to think about the fact that once again my womanhood was getting stolen from me. I took a deep breath and made a decision. I was going to put on a good show, and then let a round off into his big-ass head. I opened my legs, allowing him to have all access to me, and a pleased look spread across his face.

"If you're going to kill me anyways, I might as well enjoy this shit," I told him, playing with my pearl.

Coopa licked his lips as he watched my panties moisten.

"Damn, shorty," he said, kissing my inner thigh.

He moved my panties to one side and let his tongue explore the depths of my treasure. My hands ran over his smooth head as I relished in the feeling of his warm tongue slipping and sliding, tasting my sweet nectar. A few moans escaped my mouth, and he stopped suddenly, shaking his head.

"This shit, it too wet. Turn around; let me get this pussy from the back," he said.

I must have been going too slow because he grabbed my ankles and flipped me over himself, putting me at a perfect angle on the queen-sized bed to reach down and grab my clutch.

OK, Sadie, now you just have to play your fucking cards right, I thought knowing the ball was now in my court.

The feeling of Coopa ramming his monster all up inside of me interrupted my thoughts. My walls instinctively clenched tightly. Coopa proceeded to beat my love spot into ecstasy. He was giving it to me so good I even began throwing it back at him. I looked over my shoulder at him and saw how infatuated he was with my ass.

"Damn, ma, you got a fat-ass fuck! Why you have to be that nigga's people? I could've made you my shorty!" Coopa threw his head back while he rode me until I felt myself about to explode.

"Fuck, I'm about to coooome!" I couldn't help crying out.

I couldn't hold back anymore, and my body quivered violently with the intensity of my orgasm. Coopa had my juices dripping all over him, but he still wasn't ready to bust.

Fuck, I have to get this nigga to nut! I thought.

I started to make my ass clap as I threw it back at him, hoping that would be enough to make him bust.

"Hell yea, take this dick! Oooh, shit!" Coopa gripped my hips tightly, and I finally felt his dick pulsating inside of me. "I'm about to . . . ahhh!"

Coopa pulled out of me and squirted what seemed like a gallon of semen onto the bed. While he was busy enjoying the feel of his nut, I used that as my window of opportunity to reach down and grab my clutch. Although my legs were shaking, and I could barely stand, I knew what had to be done.

"Well, bitch, it was fun." Coopa wiped his hands on the bedsheets and reached for the .45 he must have set on the ground while he was fucking me. "It's a shame I have to kill you now."

The second he took his eyes off me to grab his gun was the second I used to aim mine. I let one round off, catching him by surprise in the arm. The force of my bullet caused him to drop his gun and fumble back.

"Ahh!" Coopa cringed, gripping his arm in pain. "Bitch!"

"The fuck did you think was going to happen here?" I said, standing there in just my panties and tank top. "Did you think you were going to fuck me, kill us, *rob* us, and live to tell the fuckin' tale?"

I let out a crazed laugh at the sight of Coopa standing there weighing his options. He knew he'd lost, and the realization he was feeling made me happy.

"Nigga, I'm a Last King! We don't fuckin' die!" I raised my gun again, feeling the power in my words. "You know what your mistake was, Coopa? You got too *fuckin'* comfortable, and the streets got hungry. We're here because you lost your boss mentality, and because of you, Detroit seems weak. We're here because you failed to do your job, but I guess it's good that we're here to take your place . . . huh?"

Coopa tried desperately to make a quick grab for the gun around his ankle, but I pulled the trigger one more time, rocking him to sleep forever.

"Bitch," I spat and kicked his dead body.

After I put my pants back on, I opened the door to the bedroom as quietly as I could. The television in the living room was on loudly, and that explained why they didn't hear the bullets that had just killed their boss.

"Stop!" I heard Mocha cry out over the television and snickers in the background as I eased closer to the living room. "Get the fuck off me, you dirty dick-ass niggas!"

I closed my eyes quickly trying to envision who all was in the room. There was one big black nigga and two fair-skinned skinny niggas. From their movements, I could tell that they were all in one area of the living room. I knew they were strapped, but I didn't give a fuck. I would take many bullets for Mocha if they hurt a hair on her head. I took a deep breath and slid into the room, gun raised. As soon as I entered the room, my finger clicked the trigger, catching one of the skinny guys in the chest. He dropped like a fly. They'd been in the middle of trying to pin Mocha down and pry her legs open. The turquoise Fendi dress that she'd decided to wear would have given them easy access, but from the looks of it, they were having a pretty tough time.

"What the—" the big one started.

"Fuck?" I finished for him and cold-bloodedly splattered his brains throughout the room with two bullets.

His fat ass needed two bullets to send him to the afterlife. I felt a bullet whiz past my head and saw that the last guy had time enough to get a shot off. However, Mocha kicked him, throwing off his aim. She then pulled her hidden pistol from her thigh and emptied the clip into his head. When she was done, his head was no longer on his body. Instead, it was in little bloody pieces scattered everywhere in the room.

"Stupid bitch!" Mocha kicked the bodies of the fallen as her body shook uncontrollably.

She made her way to where I stood and embraced me. Then she pulled back and examined me.

"Did he—"

"Yes," I answered her truthfully before the question fully formed from her mouth.

"Are you—" she stared again.

"I'm fine," I told her, walking to the couch and grabbing one of the two duffle bags of drug money. "Grab that shit. We gotta go."

Mocha understood that it wasn't the time or the place to get sentimental and obliged to my orders. I grabbed everything they'd taken from us and noticed I had a shitload of missed calls, all from Ray and Adrianna. I was about to call Ray back when Mocha and I rushed out of the apartment, but just as I hit the last number, I saw Ray's Escalade pull in front of the building. He jumped quickly from the driver's side and rushed to us.

"Say, you coo? Y'all good?" he asked. Worry drenched my cousin's handsome face.

I embraced him tightly to let him know that I was all good. When I pulled back, I looked into his eyes and smirked lightly.

"Go see for yourself," I told him, throwing the duffle bag into the back of his truck.

Nodding my head to the apartment, I stepped out of the way so Ray could go check out the murder scene. Adrianna, who'd been making sure Mocha was OK, quickly followed suit, wanting to see what had gone down. When Ray came back out, he wore a huge grin on his face, and I knew he was pleased with the death of Detroit's old kingpin.

"Straight like that?" Ray asked, extending his hand.

I nodded my head and shook his hand, grinning.

"Like that."

Ray's grin slowly turned into a frown as he stared into my eyes.

"That nigga ain't have no pants on, Say." His eyes pierced into mine, but I couldn't look away. "What the fuck happened up there?"

I knew he would be scoping for a lie, and I couldn't tell him what really happened. I could already see guilt forming on his face. He was blaming himself for the whole ordeal. I thought carefully about my words before delivering a story. I glanced at Mocha as if to say, *"Go along with this shit,"* before I started speaking.

"As soon as Mocha and I walked in, it was on and popping. They off'd our man before we even got there. Coopa was talkin' beef shit and was plannin' on takin' the money after he did what he wanted with me." I took a breath before I continued seeing the vein slowly throbbing on his temple. "He took me to the back room, and he had three other niggas there makin' sure Mocha's ass ain't go nowhere."

"They unstrapped you?" Ray asked.

"Yea, but the dumb nigga never took my clutch," I told him.

Ray shook his head at Coopa's stupidity.

"As soon as he dropped his pants. I pulled my gun out and blasted his ass." I tasted salt as the lie rolled off of my tongue. "Then we finished the niggas off in the living room. This murder shit is pretty gangster. I could really get used to this."

Despite the fact that we'd almost died, Mocha stifled a laugh at my joke, but Ray stood firm and serious.

"This ain't shit to joke about, Sadie! I should have never sent y'all to handle this shit! That nigga thought he was smart. You could have fuckin' died and—"

"But I didn't!" I reassured my cousin. "Kings don't die; they live on forever."

Ray looked lovingly into my eyes, and I knew why he was trippin' so hard. We grew up with only each other, until Mocha came along. If anything happened to me, I knew Ray would go insane, and vice versa. He nodded his head, agreeing with my words.

"You right. Kings don't die. The important thing is that bitch nigga is finally out of the picture." Ray grabbed the duffle bag from Mocha and handed it to Adrianna.

Ray and Adrianna got into his Escalade to take the money to where it was supposed to go. He instructed us to go directly back to his penthouse and wait for him there. Mocha and I got into her BMW 335i. I knew a sweeper team would be there soon to clean up the mess and take Coopa's body to his home front. The message would be clear. Coopa's reign was over. The reign of The Last Kings was in Detroit now. It was time to make our official claim on the city.

Chapter 12

Two Years Later

After Coopa's death, the rise of The Last Kings had to be swift and accurate. There wasn't any room for fuckups. The feds were all over Coopa's operation after his body was found. The majority of his soldiers weren't prepared to answer questions and explain where the drug money came from. They took Ray in for questioning, of course, because at one point in time, he and Coopa were clearly in cahoots. But they didn't have enough on him to keep him in custody; the murder weapon was never found. If they would have even tried to hold him, he had more than enough money to get out. So they just let him go. They couldn't tie him to the murder or to the drugs and money found in Coopa's traps, but Ray knew he would have to tread softly for a while. In the streets at least.

Mocha switched her way into Lace wearing a skintight Armani one-strap dress that stopped just above her knees and held a clutch and a black folder in her hands. The sleek black of the dress clung to her body, giving the illusion that it was actually painted on. She stepped through the door, not even bothering to flash the guard the tattoo of the pharaoh on her forearm. He knew she was affiliated. Mocha smirked as he watched her step, catching every quake of her ass.

You ain't never going to taste this, boo, Mocha thought to herself as she made her way through the dim lighting of the strip club to the back. It wasn't too busy, but there was a nice crowd surrounding the stage watching the hoes twirl around on the poles.

The stairwell led to the locker room for the strippers. Mocha knew better; she wasn't going there to chill with any of those hoes. She walked past many naked women preparing for their acts and headed directly for the showers and bathroom stalls. The last stall was for the handicapped, and on the door it read, "OUT OF ORDER," but Mocha entered it anyway. She pulled a set of keys from her clutch purse and opened the tampon box that was on the wall above the toilet paper. Instead of tampons inside it, there was a keypad in which Mocha entered a code that consisted of six numbers. Once the last number was entered, she heard a soft click and light hum. Before her, the concrete wall the toilet was attached to opened just a crack, enough for her to reach her hand through and open it the rest of the way. She walked through it, entering the secret and only trap house of The Last Kings. Ray had learned from Coopa's mistakes and knew the location of his trap had to be ducked off and out of the way.

Mocha walked down one more flight of stairs before entering a long hallway. At the end of the hallway was a high door, and on the outside of it, two big niggas stood guard. They opened the door for her before she'd even gotten all the way to them, and she nodded when she walked through. Almost immediately, she was hit with the aroma of cocaine being cut up and bagged before she saw the bitches in Victoria's Secret lingerie dealing with the product, cutting and bagging it. They wore masks over their mouths and noses to protect them from the debris. In front of each of them on the tables lay a pistol. Mocha didn't even acknowledge the bitches and went to the back room. She'd just made a big business investment, and she had come to wrap up some loose ends with Tyler. She opened the door to the basement and traveled down the stairs to where she knew Tyler was.

"Y'all gotta show these niggas that fear don't live in ya' fuckin' hearts," Tyler was instructing a room full of young men. "These niggas think we can be touched just because Coopa got merked. Fuck that!" He went and grabbed one of the young men's arms and held it up, showing everyone the tattoo of a pyramid he had on his forearm. "*This* is who the fuck we are! What we do is make this money, branded for life; one way in, one way out. If you got this fuckin' tattoo, that means you're in this shit forever. We are family, y'all, not just soldiers. But cross this team, and I will put a hollow tip in ya' fuckin' head like you was just some random muhfucka on the street. Y'all hearing me?"

Mocha stood back listening to Tyler's speech that he was giving and noticed Adrianna and Devynn standing behind him. Mocha knew that anyone in that room had to be a cold-blooded killer. They couldn't afford to have any bitch niggas on their team. Bitch niggas were the same as snitch niggas, and The Last Kings were allergic to those. Leaning on the wall, she admired the respect that was held in the room. A nigga would have to be a fool if he didn't respect Tyler. It was true he was a loose cannon, but if you showed loyalty to him, then he would be loyal to you.

This is really us, she thought, pleased, watching the hungry looks of the niggas in the room. It was a fact that she was very skeptical about the whole operation; she wasn't a killer. At least that's what she thought before she pulled the trigger of her newfound best friend. It was surprising to her how easily she could take a life. The money was the motive, and if a body was in her way . . .

well . . . Tyler noticed Mocha standing behind the crowd of niggas in the room and dismissed them all.

"What's up, ma?" he said coming up on her. His hair was freshly cut into a fade, and his facial hair was neatly trimmed. He wore Ralph Lauren from head to toe. The Rolex and diamonds shining from his ears let off that he was straight hood, even though he carried himself like royalty.

Mocha smiled at her business partner, seeing the imprint of the .45 through his shirt.

"Kings stay strapped at all times, even in their own house," Ray always said.

"Business as usual; don't act brand-new, Tyler," she told him, rolling her eyes slightly. He knew that would be the only reason she would even come to the trap. "Where's Ray?"

"That nigga is handlin' business as usual," he smirked, having fun being an asshole to Mocha who had become like a little sister to him. "What you got for us though, shorty?"

Mocha was slightly disappointed that Ray wasn't there. She wanted to see the pleased look on his face when she told him they'd come up on $200,000. She liked when he looked at her the same way he did Sadie. The only difference was that Sadie didn't have to do anything to get that look. Ray was proud of her regardless. Mocha often felt tiny pings of jealousy when it came to their relationship. Although they only had each other and Grandma Rae, that was more family than she'd ever had. Mocha's mother forced her to move from Atlanta in junior high, and then left her when she was in high school. She sent her to school with a note that said:

I ain't comin' back for this little bitch; y'all can keep her!

That was when Grandma Rae had taken her in. Sadie didn't even have to ask her, and Grandma Rae acted as if Mocha had been staying there all her life. Mocha knew she had no reason to feel that green bitch, especially when Ray did everything in his power to make her feel at home. If she needed anything, he had her, and she loved him like the big brother she never had.

"Nothin' much; just made a deal, that's all." She handed him the red folder she had in her hands with the details of the drop to be made.

"Damn, shorty! Two hundred stacks!" Tyler said, obviously pleased. "That's real nigga shit."

He grinned down at Mocha, causing her skin to blush a bit. She shrugged her shoulders as if to say, "It was nothing."

Tyler was sexy. No, Tyler was sexy as fuck. But she wouldn't dare try to get his attention for three reasons. Tyler was a loose cannon, which was the reason he was perfect for the job of Ray's general. He thought with his trigger finger and his body pile had added up quite drastically over the years. He was ruthless, and mercy was something that he knew nothing about, so it was impossible to show it. The second reason, although she thought Mocha didn't know, Sadie had some type of feelings toward him. Mocha didn't know what had happened, but she knew for a while when they were in high school, all Sadie spoke about was Tyler. But then one day it just stopped. Sadie never spoke about it again, and since then, the way she was with Tyler was different. Even now, Sadie kept everything strictly business with him, but Mocha didn't press for details. Her girl had the right to her privacy, just like she did. The last reason was because she had a love interest already. And she wasn't thinking about any other nigga.

"I had to bring something big in, since I'm going to be gone for a minute," she told him.

"Where you going? Atlanta again?" Tyler asked knowingly.

Mocha nodded her head.

"Yea, I've just been feeling a little homesick that's all," she lied through her teeth.

Tyler, however, didn't catch her lie; instead, he closed the folder in his hands, letting her know that as soon as Ray made it in, he would have him handle that.

"Cool, stay up," she said and prepared to make her departure. She raised her arm that had The Last Kings brand that only she, Tyler, Ray, and Sadie had. Tyler raised the same arm in farewell, and with that, Mocha exited the basement.

She checked her watch as soon as she was back in her new BMW and saw she only had four hours until her flight to Atlanta.

"Fuck!" she said aloud, not wanting to miss the only connection she had to her love.

She hadn't told anyone the real reason why she'd been taking so many trips to Atlanta. She couldn't tell Sadie. She wouldn't understand why she hadn't told her about him after all the time that had passed. Mocha had been seeing him ever since her field trip to an Atlanta college campus when the two were still in college. She smiled as she reflected on her first meeting with Khiron . . .

"This club is wack!" Mocha whined to Jaylin who was supposed to be showing her a good time and not boring her.

Mocha was from Atlanta so she knew something had to be wrong if the club wasn't popping.

"That's because the party isn't here yet; now chill and enjoy this drink that old nigga bought for you!" Jaylin said, laughing, acknowledging the drink in front of

Mocha. The man who sent it tipped his hat at them, and the two of them fell into a fit of giggles.

Jaylin was cool people and upon their first greeting in the dorm room she and Mocha shared, Mocha knew she could fuck with her all day. She was two years older than Mocha and quickly took her under her wing. Like Mocha, Jaylin was known to turn heads. Her chocolate skin, natural curls, and wide hips made it hard to miss her. When she walked by, all eyes were on her ass and drool was likely to hit the floor. She had the looks of a model standing at five foot seven; she was probably the baddest bitch on her campus.

She scoped Mocha out based off of her looks and decided that she'd never seen a woman more beautiful, not even herself. She knew with her by her side, they'd have drinks flowing their way all night. Mocha took Jaylin's advice and chilled, realizing that at midnight it was still early for the club. After a few more drinks, Jaylin pulled Mocha out on the dance floor, and it seemed as if they were the stars of the night. They moved their bodies to the sound of the hottest hip-hop tracks hooked up by the DJ, and they heard several whistles.

"Them bitches getting it!" they heard a few females call out.

"Ayye! Get it, bitch!" Jaylin said to Mocha as she shook her ass.

Both girls had decided to go with minidresses. However, Jaylin's was a black tube top and Mocha's was teal with sleeves and a lace cutout on the back. The heels she chose to wear made her ass sit up just right in her dress, causing it to shake viciously whenever she twerked. Mocha was enjoying herself so thoroughly she didn't even witness the entourage of twenty niggas enter the club. Her hands were in the air, and she had just started to get it to Ciara's voice coming out of the speakers when she felt a hand on *the small of her back. She turned around to slap whoever had fucked up her groove but stopped when she realized she was staring into the sexiest pair of hazel eyes she'd ever seen. She caught herself quickly though before the nigga could see her get all googly-eyed and shit.*

"Excuse you," she said and rolled her eyes rudely.

"Naw, excuse you, ma," he smiled cockily down at her from his six foot two build. "You in my city dancing like you ain't got no man, so I thought I'd fix that problem."

Mocha had to admit, dude was sexy as shit! Although she usually went for the chocolate guys, she had to admit he was one of the sexiest men she'd ever seen in her life. He had to be mixed with something, she could tell by the curls that were neatly on top of his head. When he smiled, she could see two deep dimples and a perfect white smile. She gave him a once-over and decided that if it weren't for his cocky-ass attitude, he might have been worth her time. He was dressed in a True Religion fit with a pair of the newest Js out. About one hundred thousand dollars' worth of diamonds rested on his wrist.

"Naw," Mocha said peeping his game, "I think you have me confused with one of these sloppy females in this bitch."

Mocha knew by the thirsty stares the women in the club were giving, the man standing before her must be a hot commodity in Atlanta. She didn't even notice the two goons he had standing behind him as he talked to her. She didn't care though. No matter how big he was, he looked like the type who thought he could have whatever he wanted, and Mocha refused to be one of those obtainable items. She turned back to Jaylin who had stopped dancing and was looking shocked at Mocha. She couldn't believe she was dissing a boss like the one who stood before her.

"My feet are a little tired," she told Jaylin. *"You wanna go take a seat?"*

She nodded, but before she even answered, Mocha was walking past her through the overly crowded dance floor. Mocha added an extra swish in her step, just in case eyes were watching all the way to a vacant table.

"Mocha!" Jaylin exclaimed as soon as she caught up. *"What the fuck, girl? Do you know who that is?"*

"Clearly a hustler," Mocha waved her hand in the air. *"That nigga looks like he's used to just coming to any club and picking his victim. Fuck that."*

"Bitch, so the fuck what? That's Khiron, girl! That nigga is a walking bank. Since his daddy got popped awhile back, he's been on. Running the city like a fuckin' boss since age nineteen," Jaylin said giving Mocha the spill on Khiron while Mocha tried not to trail his every move in the club. *"And let me be the first to tell you, I ain't never seen that fine muhfucka approach a bitch at a club."*

She emphasized the word *"never"* to let Mocha know she'd made a big mistake by ignoring Khiron's advances. Mocha just rolled her eyes at her.

"Bitch, I don't give a fuck. I'm only here for a fuckin' weekend, and then back to Detroit I go!" Mocha tried to sound uninterested, but in all honesty, what she'd just heard sparked her attention.

Mocha studied Khiron from where she sat, and whenever they were close to connecting eyes, she shifted her gaze. It was going quite well . . . until he tricked her by doing a double take. For ten seconds, they stared at each other from across the club through a small window that the mass number of bodies provided.

"You feeling him," Jaylin told her when she stood up to dance with a guy who'd grabbed her hand. *"Once-*

in-a-lifetime chances are only once in a lifetime. Make your move!"

Mocha sighed when her newfound friend was whisked away on the dance floor.

"Fuck it," she said under her breath and a flash of Antwan back home came to mind. "That nigga is probably fuckin' some hood rat right now anyway."

Mocha stood up and slowly made her way to where Khiron sat in the VIP section of the club. As soon as she got a little too close for comfort, one of his goons stopped her with a hard hand to her chest.

"Aye, chill, she's coo people," Khiron said to the man and waved me over to sit on the couch next to him.

"I think we got off on the wrong foot," Mocha flashed her sexiest smile at him.

Might as well go for the dick, she thought to herself as she watched him wet his lips with his tongue. This nigga is sexy as fuck!

"Naw, I feel you, ma, and I actually respect you more for saying fuck me the first time," he said pouring her a drink.

"I'm only nineteen," Mocha told him truthfully. "I don't drink. But if you have some kush I'll surely blow some with you."

Khiron was shocked to find out her age, especially since she had the body of a grown woman, but he was pleased to hear her honesty.

"A'ight, ma," he chuckled a bit. "Maybe later, but right now, let the music fade to the back of our minds and get to know each other a little better first."

They sat in the corner of the club talking for the rest of the time they were there. Mocha was so comfortable with him, it felt as if she was talking to someone she'd known her whole life. The conversation between them flowed aimlessly, and it came to light that they had *many things in common. Before the night was over, they'd blown two blunts, and he'd even gotten her to take a shot of tequila. When it was time to leave and everybody was heading to the door, Khiron grabbed Mocha by her hand. By talking to her, he knew she'd be gone the next day to go home to Detroit, and he felt that he had to spend the night with her. Not even to get in her panties; he just wanted to spend some more time with her.*

"Come home with me tonight, ma," he said in sincerity.

"The fuck I look like?" Mocha asked, a little offended, even though she'd wanted to jump his bones since she saw him. She still didn't want to come off as an easy ho. "A fucking one-nighter?"

Khiron shook his head.

"Naw, ma, nothing like that. I just enjoy your company, that's all. We ain't gotta do nothing like that if you don't want to." He pulled her close to him so that their lips were barely touching. "Just say yes, shorty . . . please? I'll make sure you get back to the dorms safely in the morning. Just stay the night with me."

Mocha melted in his arms, and the look in her eyes gave him his answer. She couldn't say no, because in all honesty, she didn't want to. She found Jaylin in the parking lot of the club and told her she'd get a ride back to the room in the morning. Jaylin gave Mocha a knowing look.

"Be careful, niggas like Khiron are only good for one night. I saw y'all gettin' friendly over there. Don't call yourself falling for a nigga like that. It's never a good thing," Jaylin warned.

Mocha nodded her head like she was really listening. The only thing on her mind was the night she had ahead of her with a man that she had just met. Mocha went on to have the night of her life, and ever since, was hooked on Khiron.

Mocha snapped back to reality as she whipped her car as fast as she could toward the airport. Her bags were already in her trunk; they'd been packed for days.

I'm on my way, baby, she said, smiling at the thought of being reunited with the love of her life.

"Please, Khiron!" the voice of a man screamed for mercy, but no one could hear him.

Khiron stood over a man who was bound tightly to a chair with a box of matches in his hand. He'd already poured gasoline around the chair, and with one match, the man's body would go up in flames. The victim in the seat was someone Khiron had to dispose of. He knew too much and was planning to go to the FBI with information about the drug operation Khiron was running in Atlanta. After Khiron's dad got pegged because a little bitch snitched on him to the Italians, there was nothing he couldn't stand more. Snitches made the earth stink in his eyes, and the world needed to be rid of them if anyone expected to make any money.

"You were going to testify against me, my nigga? Put all my work into the dirt, huh?" Khiron laughed at the petrified expression on the man's face. Any hope for mercy was long gone. "Nigga, by the time this fire is out, there won't be a body to put in the dirt."

"Man, I'm sorry! I got a kid and a wife, man." He began to sob like a little girl, and Khiron looked at him disgustedly.

I know this pussy-ass nigga ain't start crying, Khiron thought, shaking his head. *Hell naw, and this nigga was down with my shit? I'ma have to do a sweep of my own team soon.*

"Yea, I know you got a shorty and a little son," Khiron acknowledged the man's family. "And as soon as I'm done here, both of them muhfuckas going to have lead in their fuckin' skulls! You were going to snitch on me? I'm a fuckin' boss, and you? You a bitch, and dogs get put to sleep!"

Without hesitation, Khiron lit a match and threw it on the ground by the chair. The man gave a horrendous scream as he erupted in flames, fighting against the ropes that bound him to the chair. There was no hope for him. He had no other choice but to sit there and die a horrible death. Khiron watched, satisfied that he'd finally made his mark. He'd gotten to J. Will just before the feds put him into protective custody. Khiron had ears all over the city, and once he heard that J. Will was planning on singing to the cops, he snatched him up and tortured him in the middle of nowhere, until he told him that he was, in fact, planning to testify and putting him away for good. The feds had been hot on Khiron after he caught a body outside of a local strip club. It was a rookie move, but the nigga stepped, and Khiron made him fall. The feds couldn't link the body to him because no one would testify, and one of his goons disposed of the murder weapon within minutes of the crime. Khiron felt his cell phone vibrate on his hip. He smiled slightly seeing it was from his own shorty.

Hey, baby! I'm here, and I'm wearing that color you like.

Khiron grinned, knowing Mocha was probably laid out butt-ass naked in his bed because the color he liked was her mocha skin tone. He'd waited a month to get a taste of that, and he wasn't going to let a bitch-ass snitch waste any more of his time.

Handlin' some business, ma. I'ma be there as soon as I'm done. I love you.

He placed his phone back on his hip after sending his message and spit into the literally screaming fire. Then he went and got in his black Range Rover that was parked in the grass, taking one last look at the fire.

"Burn, bitch," he said and drove in the direction toward home where his lady was waiting for him.

Chapter 13

Ray walked through the silent halls of his estate toward Sadie's wing. After Coopa sent his goons to his last home, he took every precaution to ensure that nothing like that would ever happen again. He had his 80,000 square foot home built quickly and in secret. His home was unlisted in any phone book or GPS. The only way to get there was to know exactly where it was. As a boy growing up, he went on many adventures that took him far from home. The land Ray purchased to build his home was discovered during one of those adventures. It was surrounded by nothing but trees and a large, beautiful pond. The home was ducked off and out of the way of mankind, but still, as a safety precaution, he had cameras on the outside of the house and large gates around it. Ray also had two of his hired hands at the front of the gate every hour of the day. He knew that he would be gone often on business and wanted to be certain that Mocha and Sadie would be well taken care of while he was away.

Ray had housekeepers to help out and keep things orderly around the place. They had their own rooms and free reign of the home, everywhere except their bedrooms and his office. Mocha and Sadie each had their own wing in the house, but when they were both home, you could always find them together. Currently, however, Mocha was gone on a trip to Atlanta and had been gone for a little over a week. He'd checked up on it and found that she had business there and was bringing home big sums of money. He respected her grind and trusted her even more for bringing the money to their business instead of being snake about it.

Ray knocked lightly on Sadie's tall double doors once he arrived.

"Come in!" her voice called on the other side.

He entered a room fit for a queen and quickly spotted her sitting in her window seat. Sadie's room was like a large suite, kitchen and all. If she never wanted to leave it, she didn't have to. When his house was being built, Ray had special import and modification requirements. He wanted Sadie to feel like a bag of money whenever she went to bed and woke up. The room was draped in nothing but Versace. Without including the sixty-five-inch TV that hung on her wall, her king-sized bed and other furniture, or the two closets filled with designer clothes and shoes, he was standing in a $500,000 room.

"Hey," Sadie smiled up at him, wearing nothing but a T-shirt and a pair of skinny jeans.

Ray knelt and sat down by her feet. He studied her face and couldn't believe how much she'd grown up. Her beauty was breathtaking, and he was glad that she was focused on making money and not on any niggas. A year before, she was a college student and like his kid sister. Now, sitting before him, Ray could see the difference. A major difference, and he knew why. She'd taken a life . . . a few lives, actually. Ray noticed that the innocent blind-to-the-world look was gone from her eyes, only to be replaced with a look of hunger and anticipation. He couldn't see her as his little cousin anymore. At the age of twenty-one, she was a grown woman and clearly knew how to handle herself.

Sadie flipped her work faster than anyone he'd ever seen. Although he taught her a few things, Sadie already knew the game like the back of her hand. Ray was feeling a little guilty. As the new boss of the city, all of attention and energy had been on moving product in and out of the city, and he hadn't had any time to spend with Sadie. They all had been staying together, but if it wasn't about business, they barely said two things to each other. Sitting there in front of her, he took his time with his words.

"We making money out here, fam," Ray said, turning to look at Sadie's gorgeous view of the pond. The sun's rays made it look blue, like the ocean. "The Last Kings . . . us."

Sadie smiled a small smile.

"The last of a dying breed," she spoke, softly turning her head away from the window ever so slightly. Her long, silky hair fell in front of her eye.

Ray reached and pushed it behind her ear and nodded. The smile he wore on his face wasn't happy; it was a sad one.

"I never wanted this life for you, Say. You were supposed to stay in school. Be a doctor or some shit, not this." He shook his head and leaned back once more. "But the fact remains that you got something that *none* of these niggas got when it comes to this game. You got the heart of a hustler."

Ray stopped as he reflected on what Grandmas Rae used to say to Sadie growing up. *"Sadie, you're Grandma Rae's special baby. Your heart is special. Make this world, don't let it make you."*

Sadie's ambition and loyalty to the game was something Ray knew he was going to need. He remembered when they were younger and Grandma Rae could only afford to put twenty dollars a month in their pockets. Sadie would take her money to the candy store and spend it all. She sold the candy at school, and like a slanger on the corner, she tweaked the prices so that the students would still buy, but so that she would also make a good profit. Since candy at school was like cocaine to a crack house, all the kids flocked to her. Soon, it was nothing to flip twenty dollars into $300 in a matter of days. Ray knew her game was tight when she started bringing shopping bags home that neither he nor their grandmother bought.

She actually got expelled from the first high school that she attended while staying with Grandma Rae. It turned out that Sadie was the head of an operation at school that sold things; nothing illegal, however. Somehow, she got her hands on a piece of paper with the schedules of every student and teacher. It also told her when and where a classroom would be vacant. She would have one of her team send out a mass text to an exclusive number of students, letting them know when and where to come to shop. Her shop was only open fifteen minutes a day to keep it low-key. Sadie had moved up from selling candy. She started selling designer clothes she purchased on sale with the money from the original candy operation. She then sold them to all the scandalous bitches and raggedy niggas at school for the low, trying to get their stunt on. Sadie had the good shit too. Gucci, True Religion, Dior dresses, Abercrombie & Fitch, etc. You name it, and for the right price, Sadie got it.

Ray was beyond impressed when he overheard his grandmother and uncle discussing it one night. She, single-handedly, started her own business at school and was bringing in a minimum of $5,000 a week. Ray had that in mind the day he handed her that pistol. If she could flip work like that at age sixteen, he could only imagine what she could do with cocaine. The need to make money burned a fire in her eyes, and Ray knew that she was a valuable asset to The Last Kings and to himself. Out of all the six businesses, she was bringing in the most money, effortlessly. Ray knew at that very moment, Sadie was making a $150,000 deal, but she didn't feel as if that was enough money for her to show her face, so she did a conference call and had the money wired. Some of their soldiers were going to be making the drop. The way she moved her work was impeccable. Ray was a real nigga, so he could admit how crucial losing Sadie would be for his business. He also knew that out of everyone, including Tyler, Sadie was the one he could trust with everything. He knew this because they shared all of the same values, and he knew *that* because he instilled them in her.

"I've been so wrapped up in this shit that I haven't even taken the time to ask you how you've been." Ray shook his head, disgusted with himself.

"Naw, you're good," she reassured him. "We've all been busy, even Mocha. This cartel has to be strong. You never know when a hating-ass nigga is going to try to go to war. We have all the time in the world to spend time; right now, it's about getting this money the best way we know how."

Ray smiled at Sadie's words and nodded once in respect. Unlike most people, Sadie got it. She understood the way of life when cocaine was involved. You got no time off. Unless your cousin ran the whole city. The Last Kings ran Detroit, and over the last year, the city saw more money than it had in ten years.

"I feel you on that." Ray reached in his pocket and grabbed something out. "But every boss needs a break."

He handed Sadie the contents in his hand, and when she saw what they were, her face lit up.

"Jamaica? Oh my God!" Sadie's eyes widened as she looked at the tickets.

"The perfect place to let loose, lay low, and have a good fuckin' time," Ray told her, reminiscing on his trips to Jamaica. "And it will give me a chance to pick ya mind a little."

"When are we going?" she asked, rolling her eyes although the effect was thrown off by the big smile on her face.

Ray smiled mischievously and took the tickets back.

"Pack your bags, shorty, our flight leaves in the morning."

Chapter 14

My bags were packed in less than two hours, and I barely got any sleep. I was too ecstatic to be leaving the country. Never in my twenty years of life did I think I would ever get such an opportunity. The fact that Ray was placing it at my feet brought me even more joy. I was a little upset that Mocha wouldn't be joining us, but that was cool. I knew she was doing her thing in the A and getting that Last Kings money. Early the next morning, my personal housekeeper Maria assisted me with waking up and getting dressed. She was a tiny, older woman, and she put me in the mind of Grandma Rae. Ray tried to get her to move in with us, but she declined, insulted. She had owned her house for more than thirty years and wasn't going to give that up. So having Maria was a good thing on my part, especially since she treated me with the kindness and love a grandmother would give a granddaughter. After the last bag was placed inside of the Hummer limo parked outside of the house, I gave her a big hug, knowing it would be a week before I saw her again.

"Maria?" I said into her hair.

"*Sí, señora?*" Maria said, releasing me, holding my hands.

"Do me a favor and don't do any work for the next week." I smiled big because she and I both knew that wasn't going to happen.

Maria gave a big laugh.

"Señora, working is in my blood," She looked lovingly into my eyes. "*You* do me a favor and have a good time, OK?"

I nodded, and with one last hug, I let the driver open my door, and I climbed in the limo across from Ray. The limo was decked the fuck out with a TV and a minibar. I was thinking *OK! I'm feeling this!* Even though I drove an all-black Range Rover, I was still loving the luxury.

"You ready?" Ray asked, cheesing and rubbing his fingers on his goatee.

"I'm ready," I smiled at him feeling the butterflies in my stomach. "I've never been on a plane before."

"Well, there's a first time for everything, right?" he asked me and motioned for the driver to pull off.

I turned to look out the tinted window at Maria once more. I knew she couldn't see me, but she waved nevertheless as the limo pulled off. I smiled and leaned back in my seat, knowing that ahead of me lies a beautiful paradise.

"I gotta go holla at Tyler before we hit the airport," Ray told me.

"Cutting it close, don't you think?" I asked, wary that we could potentially miss our flight.

"We'll be coo," he turned to the right slightly and yelled to get the driver's attention. "Pierre! Make a stop at Amore!"

I watched Pierre, a little African man, tip his hat acknowledging Ray's words. He drove us through the woods and finally we reached a highway. We had two hours before our flight left, and we had to be there an hour before. Pierre got us to Amore in less than fifteen minutes. That nigga was flooring the gas to get us there in a timely manner.

I stared at the outside of the building I saw daily and felt a twinge of pride. I ran it day in and day out. Unknown to any federal agency, Amore saw a minimum of $200,000 daily. As the heart of The Last Kings, I had to make sure business was conducted regularly. Ray told me that Tyler would be overseeing the business while we were away, but I was a little worried just because no one knew how to run it better than me. I knew the clients like the back of my hand. I guess all of those research papers in college I did had some purpose in my life after all. I dug so deep into those muhfuckas' files, I knew what hand they wiped their asses with and why. No one was going to get over on me or shut my shit down. The women I had working the club below were superb; no blemishes could be found on their bodies. They all had attributes to make the eyes of any man pop and were all nationalities. I didn't consider myself a pimp or a madam or whatever the fuck they were called nowadays. The women who worked for me were women who had nothing and nobody to depend on *but* us. They were orphans . . . rejects. Like me, but not like me at all. I purchased a nice house for them all to live in, and I paid them well. So well that none of them would ever even think to be the birdie to chirp to any fed-ass nigga. There was only one rule . . . One way in, no way out. Once you were down with The Last Kings, you got branded for life. The pyramid on their bodies showed their allegiance to us, and if they ever wanted to stop working in the club at Amore, then they could, but they would have to put in work in another part of the operation. If they wanted *out*, then my .48 would see to it that that happened.

"I'm coming in," I told Ray as Pierre opened our door. I needed to see firsthand my shit was going to be taken care of.

Ray smirked and shook his head.

"Everything is going to be straight, Say." He knew exactly why I wanted to go in.

"Yea, whatever. I need to see this shit for myself," I said, exiting the limo before he could.

"We'll be right back, Pierre," Ray said and walked quickly after me.

I entered the restaurant, and once we were spotted, we received an array of love.

"Ms. Sadie! How are you today?"

"You look fabulous!"

"Ray, my man! Looking like a sack of money, but what's new?"

We smiled and greeted everyone from servers to customers. Although it was an Italian restaurant with mostly Italian customers, our faces had become implanted into the foundation of the place. Ray's business with the Italians was proving to be the best partnership, and I truly felt like I was surrounded by family.

We walked to the secret entrance of the club and found Tyler in the money room, of course. He was looking fresh as usual in Ralph Lauren from head to toe. The fade on his curly head was fresh, and he gave me a knowing look once he saw me.

"I should've known yo' ass wasn't going to leave without stopping by," Tyler said smirking at me smugly as he finished rolling a joint.

I gave him a sideways glance and made my way past him to look at the counts so far, but before I could get to them, he stepped in front of me. His Ralph Lauren cologne invaded my nostrils, and I stopped in my tracks although I was not able to stop the butterflies from fluttering in my gut.

"Everything is coo, ma; don't trip," he said seriously.

"Move out of my way, Tyler," I said trying to sound rude.

"Put them fuckin' claws away, Say," Ray said, chuckling. "My man is only doing what I asked. You on vacation, shorty; you been working nonstop since you been on. Tyler is going to hold down the spot for you starting now."

"But—" I was cut off by Ray's hand being held up, and I knew it would be futile to argue; instead, I rolled my eyes in defeat.

"So what's real, my nigga?" Ray asked Tyler.

"We got a business proposal," Tyler said simply, and my interest piqued.

Ray was used to hearing those words, so his demeanor didn't change. He was on an uprise and there was a handful of young men who were hungry and trying to get put on. Ray turned all of them away. You had to be chosen to be down with his operation. I wondered at times if I wasn't family if he would have taken such a leap of faith with me and Mocha.

"All right, so what's up?"

"I ain't really wanna tell you right now since you about to be on a trip and shit," Tyler shrugged, and I knew he could really give two fucks about our trip; money came first. "Dude from Atlanta hit me up, says he's looking for some big work. I told him we got it, but if it ain't legit business, we can't fuck with 'em. Also told 'em he has to go through the big man first. You."

I studied Ray's face. From the sounds of it, someone was looking at Ray to be their connect. That would be a first. Ray mainly sold to clients and those residing in his area. When it came to getting his business in other cities, Ray did it himself, and he headed those operations too.

"Who is it?" Ray asked.

"The nigga's name is Khiron. He's hot in the A, I guess," Tyler told him.

"Yea, I heard of that nigga. His pops used to push some heavy work back in the day. He was on some Coopa shit, though, and ended the same way." Ray nodded his head. "If that nigga is anything like his pops, I won't fuck with it."

Tyler nodded his head, agreeing.

"I did some research on the little nigga, though, bro." Tyler sat down and leaned back in his chair. "He's bringing in mad work in the A. Word on the street is that his connect just got bumped up. Nigga is looking at life with no chance of ever seeing the outside world again."

Ray's dreads shook slightly as he cocked his head, interested.

"So the nigga is thirsty. I feel him. How much he throwing?"

Tyler sparked his joint and took a long draw from it.

"Here's the fuckin' kicker, bro." He sat forward rubbing his light hand across his face. "He wants to talk business. Face-to-face, he wants to do some big business with us. I guess he heard what The Last Kings is doing in the dope game and wants a slice of this pie. Only thing is the kind of pie and how big his slice is, is up to you."

"A'ight, and when does he want to conduct his business?" Ray asked.

I looked at Tyler as he fixed his mouth to speak, knowing what he was about to say before the word was out.

"Tomorrow," Tyler said, grinning sheepishly.

I rolled my eyes and looked at Ray. My visions of paradise quickly faded away. Business always came first. I knew that, but I couldn't lie and say I wasn't a slight bit disappointed. I tried to remove the disappointment from my face, but Ray still saw it.

"A'ight," Ray said, running his fingers through his dreads the way he did when he was deep in thought. "I'ma hold down shit here, Tyler; you're going to go in my place to Jamaica, fam. It's only a week."

Both Tyler and I looked at him, and then at each other. What Ray was informing us was that he wanted Tyler to accompany me overseas. Alone. The look in Tyler's eyes said he didn't think it was a good idea, and the butterflies in my stomach agreed.

"Are you sure, fam? You might need me here," Tyler said, still looking at me.

"For what?" Ray asked picking up a stack of hundreds and holding it up for us to see. "The flow of this shit never stops. Go. Pierre is waiting. He has the plane tickets."

I broke eye contact with Tyler and smiled at Ray.

"Thanks, fam. Just don't burn this bitch down while I'm gone," I whispered into his ear, giving him a hug.

"Watch after her and make sure she has the best time possible. You feel me?" Ray said with one good squeeze, and then let me go.

Tyler stood up and shook Ray's hand.

"You know it," Tyler said. "Well, let's go then, shorty. We don't want to miss *our* flight now, do we?"

I cut my eyes at him and gave Ray one last farewell before leading Tyler to the limo.

"I was starting to think you weren't coming back," Pierre said, opening my door.

"No, I'm definitely going, but there has been a slight change in plans," I said nodding my head backward to Tyler. "Ray's staying, but this nigga is coming."

"This nigga?" Tyler said in his deep voice laughing. "What's up, Pierre? Just try to get us to the airport in one piece."

"Will do," Pierre smiled at the two of us and winked at me.

I didn't know what that was all about, but it was almost like he knew something I didn't. He shut the door behind us and once he climbed in himself, we were on our way. Tyler sat across from me, and I couldn't help but notice how handsome he was. His mother was a white woman, and his daddy was black as night. The mixture of the two gave him a nice smooth light brown skin tone. His facial hair was perfectly trimmed and lined along his powerful jawbone structure. His eyes were hazel and cold as ice, but that came with the job. His body structure was similar to Ray's; big, muscled, and intimidating. I tried not to stare, but it was like I was seeing him for the first time in years. As my gaze traveled down to the one thing that remained hidden, his voice interrupted my almost naughty thoughts.

"Excited?" Tyler asked me, showing his perfect pearly whites.

"A little bit," I smiled at him, wondering if he'd been watching me study him that whole time.

"Shot?" Tyler went into the bar and got out a bottle of Hennessey and two shot glasses. "Real niggas drink dark liquor."

"Don't mind if I do." When I reached to grab the tiny glass Tyler had poured the liquor into, our hands brushed slightly together, and I felt a tingly feeling in the pit of my stomach. It was a feeling that I'd been fighting off for years. I had a secret. If Ray knew that secret, he may not have let me go thousands of miles away with Tyler. Tyler was like a big cousin to me, and more so, he was Ray's right-hand man from the jump, so any attraction I felt for him had to be ended.

When I was in my senior year of high school, I tried to test the waters and see how far I could get before having to resurface. I remembered that night like it was yesterday. It was the reason being alone with Tyler was more than a little awkward. Tyler used to stay the night at Grandma Rae's house all the time, and my budding crush on him had turned into a burning desire to feel him inside of me. The feelings I had for him were so real, or they seemed like it. After all of the sexual trauma I'd gone through, it was hard giving myself away to just anyone. I hated sex after Nino. I had only slept with two other guys, and I regretted both times. But for some reason, I had it in my mind that I had to have Tyler.

At that age, all the girls were on Tyler and Ray, but I had already claimed Tyler as mine. I would sometimes catch him staring curiously at me . . . not in the way a guy looked at his best friend's kid cousin. In his eyes there was a longing. We used to kick it all the time. He would pick me up from school, and we would just ride and talk about nothing, but everything. He told me that I was smart and could be anything I wanted to be in life, and I remember wanting to tell him all I wanted to be was his girl, even though I knew he would just turn my young ass away with all the grown pussy being thrown his way. He was asleep in Ray's room one night. Ray was gone. I don't remember why he was, I just remember he wasn't there. I snuck in the room after deciding that it was time for me to make my move. I blinked, and in one quick moment, my eyes shut and I reminisced on how things played that night.

He was sleeping soundly when I entered the room with nothing but my bathrobe hiding my eighteen-year-old body. I turned on some sensual R&B music and dimmed the lights to set the mood. As I stared before me, I licked my lips just at the thought of climbing on top of Tyler. The Tyler. All the girls in my class wanted a piece of that, and I was going to be the one to get it. I knew he was feeling me just by how he looked at me. I knew I'd finally grown into my body, and now was the time to put it to work.

Ray had a king-sized bed, and I softly mounted it, barely making it move as I crawled like a lioness toward her unsuspecting prey. Tyler slept shirtless and on his back, which made it easier to straddle him. I let the music take its toll on my mind-set and slowly let my robe drop, exposing my perky breasts. I was excited for Tyler to see and take me all for himself, but still, I decided to move slowly. I lowered my body and kissed his soft lips . . . just a peck. But that was all that was needed to stir him. I then let my tongue travel to his neck and to his exposed chest.

"Mmm," he moaned softly, still not yet all the way awake.

"You like that, baby?" I whispered seductively.

When he nodded his head, I leaned back in and began to kiss him passionately, and he returned it. I felt his warm hands explore every depth of my body, and my treasure began to drip with juices. His hands squeezed my ass and pinched my nipples sensually, but his eyes still did not open once. I let my hand slide down toward his briefs and massage his manhood. Feeling it in my hand made me more eager to let it slide inside of me. His dick was huge and lived up to all stories told about him. Actually, I didn't think the stories did him justice. Lowering my pelvis, I began to grind slowly to the slow beat of the song that was playing.

"Oooh, shit," Tyler breathed.

"Can I have it?" I whispered into his ear.

"Do you want it?" he asked, sticking his fingers deep inside my treasure.

I bit my lip and squeezed my walls tightly around his finger.

"Yes," I barely breathed. I couldn't believe it was about to happen, and I circled my hips on his fingers as they thrust in and out of me.

"Oh, fuck, this shit is wet, ma," he whispered into the air, eyes still shut.

Tyler gripped my waist and with one swift move, threw me on the bed with him on top of me. His strength turned me on, and my hands clawed at his body. Our lips met again, and I somehow ripped his briefs off, more than ready to be one with him. Just as he was about to enter me, his face inches from mine, his eyes opened, and I was staring into the most beautiful pair of hazel eyes I'd seen in my life.

"Say?" he said, and the horror in his voice broke my heart. "What the fuck do you think you're doing, shorty?"

He jumped up and stared at me with disgust in his eyes.

"Calm down!" I tried to hush him, not wanting to wake Grandma Rae. I wrapped the cover around my nude body, trying to hide myself.

Tyler took a deep breath and tried to calm himself.

"What were you thinking, Say?" Tyler calmed his voice down. "What if someone would have come in and saw you trying to . . . to—"

"I'm sorry," I said in a meek voice, hanging my head. "I just thought you wanted me . . . like I want you."

Tyler sighed and ran his hands over his curly fade.

"Look, Say, you're like my li'l cousin. I don't think about you like that," he said in a softer tone, probably not wanting to hurt my feelings more than he already had.

"You wanted me a second ago," I whispered.

"A second ago my eyes were closed," he said forcefully. "This is my fault, shorty. I should have never let you catch me slipping."

I just nodded my head and grabbed my robe.

"Let's just act like this never happened, a'ight?"

I didn't say a word, just got up and ran out of the room. Pretend was right. Tyler had broken my heart. I would pretend that I never had feelings for him at all.

My eyes opened, and I smiled at Tyler as he sat grown and suave before me holding up his glass.

"Cheers," he said.

"Cheers," I smiled and clanked his glass with mine.

This is going to be an interesting week, I thought with a smirk and welcomed the burning sensation as I emptied my glass.

Chapter 15

Mocha quietly climbed out of Khiron's king-sized bed in her nightie, not wanting to wake him. It was her last morning with him, and she wanted to surprise him with breakfast in bed. She tiptoed her way through his large house to his oversized kitchen and went to work. Chicken and waffles, a breakfast fit for a king! That's what he was. Her king. Mocha hadn't meant to fall in love with Khiron, but after all of the trips to Atlanta and all the time they'd spent together, it was hard not to. She felt bad for keeping secrets from him, and even more so, her team, but she felt that she was entitled to a personal life. A life no one but she could control. She also felt that it was vital to keep her affiliation with The Last Kings secret. Although he was a hustler in Atlanta, he was pulling in heavy weight in his own city. His operation wasn't moving nearly as much work as The Last Kings, and Mocha felt that would put a huge dent in their relationship if he knew. As far as Khiron knew, she was still a student working part time at a local bank. Who said a good relationship couldn't be built on a lie? Mocha also knew Khiron's temper. She'd been present for enough killings and kidnappings. Khiron was the type of man who just didn't care. Whereas Ray's heart was cold, Khiron simply didn't have one; only with Mocha. She didn't know how he would take it if he found out his girl saw more money in one day than he did in two months. She knew Atlanta was a hard market, so she had been giving them work at a lower price. She wasn't anyone's connect, but the product she provided the city kept its drug ring afloat. Mocha also knew if Khiron found that out, he would flip the script.

"*Baabbyy,*" Mocha purred into his ear once his breakfast was made and sat on a small table tray before him.

"Mmm," Khiron stirred before finally opening his eyes. Once he saw the food in front of him, a big smile crossed his face. "Damn, ma, you the fuckin' best!"

Mocha returned his smile and handed him his eating utensils. "Eat up!" she said.

And that he did. The air was filled with smacking and chewing. In less than ten minutes, the plate was completely clean. Mocha stared at the plate, shocked, wondering if the nigga had been starving.

"Damn," she said, cutting her eyes seductively at him. "With all that eating you did last night, I didn't think you'd be that hungry."

Khiron grinned and pushed the tray to the floor, causing the dishes to make a large clanking noise.

"Girl, you know I can never get enough of you. A nigga is always hungry!" He pulled her on top of him, and they shared a passionate kiss before Mocha pulled away.

"I have to hop in the shower, babe. You know my plane leaves in three hours," Mocha said.

Khiron looked at the clock and saw it read ten o'clock and remembered that her flight took off at one o'clock. He knew how Mocha was. Early was on time. He smiled at her and squeezed her bottom for good measure.

"A'ight, ma, it's coo. Leave your man lying here with a hard dick. I see how it is," he told her playfully.

Mocha rolled her eyes at him and kissed him one last time.

"Boy, your dick is always hard. What's new?" She laughed at him and got up from the bed. "You can join me if you'd like," she winked at him.

"Naw, I'm good right here." Khiron wasn't yet ready to get out of bed.

"Suit yourself." Mocha shrugged her shoulders and disappeared inside of the bathroom in the bedroom.

Once she was out of sight, Khiron sighed and shook his head. He didn't know what he was doing anymore. Mocha was meant to be only a fling, but here it was coming up on a year, and the bitch was still in and out of his crib. She was honestly the only woman that had ever even seen the inside of his home. He hadn't meant to develop such strong feelings for the girl, but he couldn't help it. She was smart, independent, and sassy, just like he liked them. Not to mention her body put even the curviest woman to shame. But Khiron also knew love in the dope game got you killed, and he wasn't ready to die. Especially not over pussy. That's how his pops went out, and he, for damn sure, wasn't going to follow in his footsteps. His dad was one of the greatest dope men to ever grace the streets of Atlanta. That man could push work in his sleep. In the end, however, he met a sticky end, just like so many before him. It was all bad for Khiron when he found that out. He was nineteen and at the age where he would have inherited all of his father's empire. Instead, all he got was a box of his father's old videos that he accidently left with Khiron's mother, his father's old machete, and a few pieces of jewelry. Khiron had to fight for his rightful place at the top and put many bodies under.

Once his pops was dead, Atlanta went crazy. Everybody was trying to be the next kingpin, even though there could only be one. Eventually, Khiron claimed his right to fame by killing any nigga in his way. Khiron watched the videos his father left behind several times, and each time got knots in his stomach. The videos clearly showed the face of the one who betrayed his father . . . someone close to him.

Too close.

Khiron swore on his father's grave that he would avenge his death once he located them, but in the meantime, he was in a sticky situation when it came to his cartel. Things were going smooth for him. His business was expanding, but after a huge drug bust, his connect wound up in prison. He got life without a chance of parole. Now, Khiron was stuck with serving a city with no fucking connect. No connect meant no money. No connect meant no cartel, and he couldn't have that. Once his well ran dry, that would be the end of the road for him, but he wasn't with that. He wasn't tripping too hard though. He knew off tops where he could find a connect. Detroit. Mocha's home. He wanted to ask her if she knew anything about The Last Kings, even though he knew she couldn't. The operation was too smooth and low-key. He knew they were getting millions of dollars. The stories he heard about them sounded like myths and urban legends, but he knew they existed, and it wouldn't be hard for him to get a number.

When Coopa was still running shit in the city, they'd crossed paths a few times to conduct business, and every time, Khiron remembered a cat by the name of Ray being there. When he first met with them, he made the mistake of shaking Ray's hand first, mistaking him for Coopa. He just had that aura about him. That man had a presence that could make any nigga bow. Not cocky, just confident, and when Khiron sent a few of his soldiers to scope out Detroit, he found that Ray was, in fact, the new boss of the city. All he needed to do was get in contact with him and get the product he needed to push in his city.

There was also another plan in the works. Detroit was a great market for business. Khiron wanted it. He didn't mention to Mocha that he would be catching a flight to Detroit a little after hers because he didn't want her all in his business or checking for him once he touched down.

So he just kept that little piece of info to himself, and if he ran into her in the city, he would just blow her off. There were many more where she came from.

"OK, I'm ready to head to the airport!" Mocha said cheerfully as she emerged through the bathroom door, a trail of steam following her.

"A'ight, shorty, let me throw on some shit and we can go," Khiron said, snapping out of his thoughts.

It's going to be hard to let all that go, though, he thought as he eyed her in a white Louis Vuitton minidress that clung to all of her curves and her red pumps.

He shook his head one time, and then proceeded to get dressed, trying not to let her see his Louis Vuitton suitcases in the closet.

Once Mocha was through the terminal, her tiny vacation was swiftly over with one phone call.

"Hello?" she said into the phone, recognizing Devynn's number.

"You back?" Devynn cut right to the chase.

"Just touched down actually," Mocha told her, throwing her suitcase to the driver of the Mercedes waiting for her in front of the airport.

"Coo, I need you to meet me at Lace tonight at nine o'clock sharp," Devynn told her.

"Any particular reason why?" Mocha asked, leaning back into the cold leather inside of the luxury vehicle.

"Well, if your ass didn't feel the need to go to Atlanta as much as you change thongs, you would know that some little niggas came into the salon this morning trying to rob it and shit." She didn't even try to disguise the annoyance in her voice.

"You coo?" Mocha asked, knowing that the salon was all her.

"The question is . . . Are them niggas coo, and the answer to that is . . . hell naw." Devynn began telling her the story, and Mocha was all ears. "It was early, so I was the only one there, of course. When I went to the back room to do some counts, I heard the window crash. It had to be at least six niggas all strapped. I got three of 'em, but real shit, if Amann hadn't decided to stop by unexpectedly, I wouldn't be alive to be talking to yo' ass."

"Damn," Mocha said, genuinely concerned. "I'm glad you're cool. What'd Ray say?"

"We think the shit was premeditated. They had to have been watching the spot close for a minute to learn its schedule, and today was a drop-off day. One hundred stacks alone were in the back room, and they would have had it all if they would have popped me."

"So what's going on at Lace tonight?"

"Bitch, we on the phone. Just be there, a'ight?" Devynn said, insinuating that the phone could be tapped.

"A'ight, where's Sadie?" Mocha rolled her eyes at Devynn's quaintness. She never really liked her, but she dealt with her just because of the business. "Is she going to be there too?"

"You don't know?" Devynn chuckled.

Mocha was confused at what was so funny but tried to keep a steady voice.

"Know what?"

"Girl, Sadie ain't here. She probably chilling on the beach somewhere topless and shit. Her and Tyler both, actually."

"Hold up." Mocha tried to make sense of her words. "What are you saying?"

"She in Jamaica, girl, for a week. She actually just left yesterday with Tyler." Devynn, once again, didn't try to hide the smugness in her voice.

Mocha, although very shocked, didn't want to give Devynn the satisfaction.

"Aw, OK, that's what's up," she said like she didn't care. But in reality, a million and one thoughts were going through her mind.

Why the fuck is Sadie in Jamaica? With Tyler especially? And why the fuck didn't she tell me she was going?

"I'll be there," Mocha said and ended the call.

Sadie kept telling her to chill when it came to Devynn, but Mocha just didn't like her. She knew to be in good with Ray you couldn't be on any snake shit, but there was something about her attitude that she didn't like. Sadie often said it was because they were so alike in many ways. Mocha didn't want to admit it, but, of course, Sadie was right. The two of them were both headstrong, which made them hardheaded. Once stuck in their own way, it was impossible making them see reason. Devynn was just cocky, and Mocha didn't like that shit. Mocha gave the driver the directions to her destination; then she sat back sipping on her Chardonnay thinking about what Sadie was up to.

"This is beautiful!" I exclaimed, leaning over the balcony from my room in the penthouse suite Tyler and I shared. "I can't believe I'm here!"

From my balcony, I had the perfect view of the beach. Although we had just returned from the sand and the joys of being swamped by the huge waves, I couldn't get over the scenery. I stood there with my towel wrapped around my waist and wet hair loosely hanging over my shoulders. I was sad that Ray wasn't there to enjoy my first trip out of the country, but I was happy that he chose Tyler to accompany me. We had so much fun at the beach. I never knew that Tyler had such a soft, fun, loving side, but he was right beside me, splashing in the water. He even dunked me a few times, hence my hair being as fucked-up as it was. We made a sand castle, and he said that it was The Last Kings mark on Jamaica. When I first emerged in my string bikini, Tyler's eyes traveled my body for a brief second, but that was the only awkward moment in the whole day. He never advanced on me as we ran around like teenagers, and I felt at peace. No killing, no guns, no drugs. I forgot what it felt like to just chill out and relax. At home I was always on edge, driving around in bulletproof vehicles and traveling with ten goons at a time. I felt at ease here, and as long as Tyler was beside me, I felt safe. I was feeling a little sad for not telling Mocha where I was, but she was in Atlanta handling business, and I didn't want to interrupt anything. She would understand.

"This is my third time being here," Tyler said coming up from behind. "Each time I come I expect it to be less beautiful than before."

"And?" I said smiling up at him.

"It's always as beautiful as before," he smiled back down at me.

I stood there and took in the man before me. He must have hopped in the shower as soon as we hit the door. My nostrils inhaled his Burberry Weekend cologne, and my eyes took in the white wife beater that hugged his muscular upper body in the sexiest way and the camouflage cargo shorts he wore. On his feet he had a pair of all-white Retro Jordan 4s and although a simple fit, I was feeling his fresh. I was supposed to be getting ready too, since we were going to head out to dinner. But I'd gotten distracted by the view. The next words out of my mouth were words I could have kicked myself for, but I couldn't stop them from escaping my lips.

"Those bitches must have been something special if you're flying them to Jamaica." I could hear the jealousy dripping from my voice.

Tyler gave a wholehearted laugh and shook his head.

"Naw, ma, you got it all wrong." He crossed his arms and turned around so that his back leaned on the balcony.

Fuck it, I thought. I'd already said it; might as well go with the flow.

"Oh, do I now?" I asked.

"Yea, you do."

"Enlighten me then," I told him.

Tyler looked at me and chuckled, shaking his head. "A'ight, ma, if you insist. You soundin' a little jealous, but I'll peep you on some shit if you can handle it," he smirked at me.

I rolled my eyes at his comment.

"Fuck you, Ty, now talk." I wrapped my towel more tightly around my waist.

"A'ight, ma, it's like this. I'm a fuckin' boss. If I feel like taking a trip, I'ma buy a fuckin' ticket. I'm never pressed for pussy, but if I have a bitch with me at the time I make my decision, then she's going be on that plane with me. If I plan on going on any trip, it's either going to be business or pleasure. If it's pleasure, I'ma fuck 'em, pluck 'em, and when we get back, I'm done with that bitch," he told me bluntly.

"I thought you said I had it wrong, as in you didn't bring bitches with you," I said smugly trying not to get mad. I mean, I didn't have a reason to be mad. He wasn't my nigga nor would he ever be.

"No, I said you had it all wrong 'cause you said they were special," Tyler said matter-of-factly, smirking at me. "And in that sense, you had it all wrong."

"Whatever, Tyler." I couldn't keep the smile from coming. "One question, though."

"What up, shorty?"

"What would you classify this as? Business or plea-sure?" I knew I was pushing it, but I threw him a sexy smile anyway and swished my way to the bathroom inside of my bedroom. Before the door shut I caught one last glimpse of him on the balcony, watching me and biting his lip.

When I was finished cleansing every crevice of my body from sand, I lotioned myself up, making it silky smooth and decided to wear a coral-colored maxi dress. It wasn't too tight and left a few things to the imagination. The top was tubed, and it stopped a few inches above my ankles. I chose a pair of nude-colored gladiator sandals and accessorized accordingly. I made the choice to match him with my fragrance, and once I pinned my still wet curly hair atop of my head in a messy white-girl type bun, I walked down the stairs of the suite to see Tyler waiting at the door for me. The smile that spread on his face was priceless.

"You look beautiful," he told me.

"I know." I showed him all of my teeth and walked through the door he held open for me. "Thanks, though."

Tyler shook his head at my cockiness.

"I have reservations at this nice spot. It has the best view of the city, and it's close enough to walk," he said as he trailed alongside me.

"You took those hoes there?" I asked bumping my hip on his playfully as we made our way through crowds of people.

"You know," Tyler said chuckling, "you need to really get that jealousy shit out cha system, ma. The shits not a good look, especially for a boss-ette."

"I'm not jealous!" I snapped. "I just don't wanna go anywhere you shared memories with your bitches."

On the strip, Tyler stopped abruptly and grabbed me softly by my shoulders.

"Sadie, chill out. We're here to have a good time and enjoy ourselves. Stop tripping. You know I wouldn't disrespect you like that. This is a spot that I actually have only come to by myself, and now I'm sharing it with you. Is that coo?"

I stared up into Tyler's eyes and saw the sincerity in them. Why he felt the need to explain was beyond my head, but I had peace of mind knowing he hadn't been up in the spot with some chickenhead. I nodded my OK and linked arms with him.

"I've been meaning to ask you something," I told him as we walked through the loud groups of natives and tourists.

The sun was going down, and it gave our surroundings a beautiful glow. I never wanted to leave, but I knew this break from business was only temporary. But I still was curious about the reason why Ray stayed behind. I wanted some info on the person he was meeting, but I was waiting for the right moment to ask. Although, for the most part, I knew everything that was going on in the operation, there were some things Ray and Tyler kept from the rest of us.

"This way," Tyler said, rounding a corner with me in tow. "What's up, shorty?"

Just as I was about to answer his question, a group of young Jamaicans, all with thick, long dreads, approached us on the strip.

"Ay, mon!" one of them said with a thick accent. "You smell like money. We dance for you, mon! And we get some?"

I looked at the five young kids and was curious of what they could do. I'd seen many strange talents on the strip, and this one looked like it would be at least seminormal.

One of them had a stereo, and he set it down to prepare the act's song.

"What's your name?" Tyler asked in his deep intimidating voice.

"Blaze," the kid said matter-of-factly, and something told me his mother didn't give him that name.

"A'ight, let's see what y'all can do," Tyler told him nodding. "But waste my time, and I'll have all you little muhfuckas regretting the shit."

The boys looked at each other somewhat nervously. An actual challenge had been placed on the table, and if they didn't beat it, there was no telling what the fuck Tyler would do. I folded my arms and stepped back to watch. As they got into their formation to start their performance, I felt a crowd slowly forming around us. The beat dropped, and once it did, they took off. I couldn't keep the smile off of my face as I watched them break dance; it gave me a rush! They were so good they should have been on that show *America's Best Dance Crew*. These little Jamaican niggas could get it! I grabbed on to Tyler's arm and squealed with joy as they did one final set of flips and ended the show. They, of course, got a huge round of applause, and Tyler himself even had a grin on his face.

"So what's up, mon?" Blaze asked out of breath.

Tyler stared them down for a moment, giving them each eye contact, before he reached in his pocket and peeled five hundred American dollars from a crisp stack of Ben Franks. He gave each of them one, and after seeing their eyes grow large, he grabbed my hand. Without another word to them, we began our journey to the restaurant once more. Seeing all that money in his hands reminded me of the question that I was meaning to ask him.

"So what's up, Say?" Tyler asked, clearly thinking about the question as well.

"That nigga trying to do business with us—"

"Khiron?" Tyler asked.

"You said he's hot in the A, right?" I asked him as we walked.

"Yea, something like that. The little nigga is on the come up."

"Why haven't I ever heard of him then? I know every hustler in every city. Why am I missing him?" I asked.

When Ray left me in charge of Amore, I did my research. Just in case a war started between us and whoever, I wanted to have every city on lock. I needed to know who the fuck was selling to whom, who was beefing, and what niggas were plotting. After a few snitching-ass niggas gave me all the info I needed on the major drug cartels in the big cities, I found that there was no one fuckin' with The Last Kings. The only one cutting close was Legacy in Miami, but that nigga wasn't stupid enough to test a nigga of Ray's caliber. See, Ray not only had The Last Kings, but he had the Italians on his side too, and *nobody* wanted to fuck with the Italian Mafia.

"That nigga been low," Tyler began to explain. "A while back, his daddy got merked by the Italians. Nigga had a bad gambling problem." Tyler shook his head. "After he died though, the empire Khiron should have inherited rightfully was dispersed to the greedy hands of Atlanta. The nigga had to practically claw his way from the bottom back to the top, which is why when he hit me up on business, I figured it was best for Ray to handle the situation."

"Why?" I asked swerving to miss a drunken couple laughing and dancing along the sidewalk.

"Because that means the nigga is hungry," Tyler said, his tone insinuating that I should already know that info. "A hungry nigga can be a good thing because that means he's ready to put in work. But a hungry nigga can also be the worst type of nigga. A hungry nigga can turn snake in a matter of seconds, and that nigga Ray can smell a snake from a mile away."

I nodded agreeing with Tyler's judgment on having Ray handle the situation. If the nigga was on snake shit, I knew he would never make it back to Atlanta . . . in one piece anyway.

"We're here," Tyler said bringing us to a stop in front of a small restaurant with all-glass windows. I was shocked because I definitely wouldn't have pegged Tyler as the type to enjoy such a place. He must have seen the expression on my face because he smiled. "I'm not too fond of these windows and shit, but the food is enough to keep a nigga coming back! Come on."

I followed him inside, and the restaurant was genuinely beautiful. I had never seen anything like it back in the States. It was jungle themed with wild, colorful plants hanging everywhere, and it even had a large fountain in the middle shaped like a waterfall. We were quickly welcomed by a swarm of gorgeous women all looking hungrily at Tyler.

"I see another reason why you come back too," I said under my breath, and he seemed not to have heard me. We were seated at a low table by a half-dressed woman.

"May I take your order?" she asked Tyler in very good English and completely ignored me.

I couldn't deny it, she was gorgeous, but I knew she for damn sure didn't look better than me. Her hair was short, and her mouth was large. She was shapely, but not proportioned well.

"What you want to drink, ma?" Tyler asked me, and I saw her roll her eyes on the sneak.

"Order me whatever," I told him smiling flirtatiously to piss her off even more. "I know you got me."

Tyler ordered us some food, ignoring the attitude the woman had suddenly started giving.

"Will that be all?" she asked sarcastically, rolling her eyes openly at me.

"Naw, shorty, but while you back there, get us a new server," he told her calmly. "You don't even know me, and you pressed for a dick that would never even entertain that big-ass duck mouth of yours. Since you're being rude to my guest, the rest of the time I'm here, I don't want to see your fucking face, a'ight?"

Tyler stared so coldly at her I swear her chocolate face turned purple before she turned on her heels and basically ran back to the kitchen.

"You better have checked that bitch," I told him, hiding my smile. "Those eyes were about to get snatched out of her fuckin' head!"

"You know I got you, ma, like you said," he replied, staring into my eyes.

I bit my lip and had to look away. The way his eyes lingered on mine made me feel something in my stomach that I hadn't felt in years. The last person to make me feel that way was, of course, the person sitting across from me. There was just something about Tyler that I couldn't shake. It had always been like that. I'd just gotten used to ignoring the feeling. But now being alone with him, it was proving difficult to not mix business and pleasure in my mind.

"Look at me," Tyler told me.

"I can't," I said truthfully.

"Why not?"

I sighed. Our vacation was only a week, and I would need a lifetime to decipher my emotions. Being around Tyler that short time was making me feel all sorts of feelings for him that I knew I shouldn't have been feeling.

"I just can't," I told him shaking my head looking at everything in the restaurant *but* him.

Without warning, Tyler reached across the table and cupped my chin gently in his hand, forcing me to look at him.

"Don't ever be afraid to look at me, ma, no matter what," he told me in a soft but stern manner.

"But I am afraid," I told him honestly.

"You weren't afraid back home," he pointed out.

"Home is different. I know what's real when I'm there, I'm protected. But here . . . It's like I'm living out my fantasies. My dreams."

Tyler stared at me, and for a brief second, the coldness that lived there disappeared, only to be replaced with a look of longing.

"You remember that night?" he asked in a low voice releasing my chin.

Of course I remember that night. Because I've spent the majority of my time the past few years trying to erase it from my memory. I didn't say that though.

"I think about that shit all the time," he kept going, and I knew I didn't want to hear what he had to say, but my ears were fixated on his words anyway. "I used to tell myself that I didn't know it was you, before I realized that it was. But something in me knew it was. I watched you grow up . . . You were like Ray's kid sister, so I just kind of adopted you as such too. But there was always something different about you, and I felt wrong for having those feelings for you. My eyes had traveled your body enough to know how it felt. And when my hands finally did touch . . . It was like heaven, ma. I wanted you so bad. Just like now. I mean, look at you. You're beautiful, and you have the mind-set of greatness. Any man would be lucky to have you on his arm. But I knew then, just like I know now, that it would never work. I can't be that man. This is business, and we can't let our personal feelings jeopardize what we have going. In this world, love is a weakness, and that's something I'm not willing to risk. You know it would never work—"

Before he could finish his statement I'd had enough. I wasn't going to sit there as he basically rejected me again. And this time, I hadn't even thrown myself at him. It felt as if my heart was being ripped out of my chest, and I couldn't handle it. Besides Ray, Tyler was the only other man I'd ever been close to, so his words cut me deep. I pushed away from the table and ran out of the restaurant, not caring that I bumped into a man carrying two trays of food and caused him to drop everything in his hands.

"Sadie!" I heard Tyler call behind me, but I ignored him.

I just wanted to get back to the safeness of my room inside of the penthouse. The vacation couldn't be over soon enough. As I ran through the crowded strip, I knew one thing was for certain. I didn't want to see Tyler until we got back to Detroit. He had killed all hope. Business was all there would be between us now.

Chapter 16

Devynn sat in the back of Lace watching the crowd go crazy over one of their best girls, Purp, wiggling her ass with little effort from her hips. The club was packed for it to be the middle of the workweek, but Devynn wasn't tripping. The more thirsty niggas, the better. She glanced around her and saw the bartenders pouring up drinks for a server to take to the VIP section of the strip club. Lace was a big thing in Detroit because, unlike Amore, which was more business savvy, the doors to Lace opened to a wider range of clients. Lace wasn't Magic City, but the bitches working there were as cold as ice. They ranged in all colors and sizes, giving Lace enough flavor needed to satisfy any man's taste.

Lace saw its share of high rollers. Whenever anybody big came to town, Lace was where they were, especially on Saturday nights. It was definitely poppin', and Devynn was feeling the vibe. The music was bumping, and every working girl was on the floor either popping their asses or their pussies in the faces of anybody with cash in their hands.

As the colored strobe lights flashed, Purp had a large audience surrounding the stage while she pranced around, dancing her heart out. Devynn stared at her and listened to the crowd go crazy when she lifted one of her legs up high, grabbed her ankle, and dropped into splits. The stage filled with money, and the bitch even picked up a few bills with the muscles of her ass cheeks, while bouncing up and down still doing the splits. Devynn's eyebrows raised, impressed with the show Purp was putting on. She averted her eyes from the stage and from the table where she was seated. With her drink, she could barely make out Adrianna in the crowd. She was making conversation with a few men at a table, who, Devynn had noticed, were being a little stingy with their wallets. She was smiling at them and laughing flirtatiously. Devynn smirked, knowing what she was doing. Adrianna was a beautiful Latina woman, and very likable. It was hard to deny her any want or need; she just had that type of personality. She was like Poison Ivy.

After a few more moments of talking to them, Adrianna grabbed two Beckys, Bubbles and Candy, for the table of men to have fun with. Devynn knew that those girls were into some freaky shit. It was a definite whenever they were put on a job, somebody's bank was going to get broken. Once they introduced themselves and made themselves at home on the laps of two of the men, Adrianna began making her way toward the table Devynn was seated at. When she saw Devynn shaking her head, she couldn't help the grin that spread across her face.

"Give them five minutes and I guarantee you, them niggas are going to be emptyin' every content in their pockets," she said proudly.

"Whateva," Devynn told her in her heavy New York accent, popping a piece of gum in her mouth.

Adrianna shrugged her shoulders, causing the half shirt she wore to raise and expose the golden sarcophagus forever branded on the side of her toned stomach.

"Where the fuck is Mocha's ass at?" Adrianna asked, looking around the crowded club to see Mocha's familiar face.

"I don't know. I told her ass to come. You know she's on her own fuckin' time." Devynn leaned back in her seat, ignoring the eyes of men staring at her.

Devynn was a beautiful chocolate-skinned woman. Her cheekbones were high, and although skinny like a model, she had a little something behind her to hold. Another drink appeared in front of her unexpectedly. She just waved it away back to whatever low-life sent it. She sipped the drink she already had, knowing that none of the thirsty men in that club would ever be lucky enough to take her home. Devynn's heart was cold as ice, and because of that, she wouldn't even entertain any of the men who had even enough guts to take a whack at any type of relationship with her. With the business she was in, she knew dating anyone was risky. Money was her only motive, and if love never came, she'd have a room full of diamonds to comfort her.

"Well, hopefully, she hurries the fuck up," Adrianna said, the look on her face implying that Mocha needed to be there.

Devynn studied Adrianna's outfit and noticed that she was a little dressier than usual. Instead of the usual skinny jeans on Adrianna's thick lower half, she wore a pair of black leggings. On her feet were a pair of badass nude pumps that crossed at the ankles. Adrianna even had a little bit of makeup on her already naturally beautiful face.

"Is Ray going to be here?" Devynn asked, and the tomato redness that overcame Adrianna's entire face was her answer. "I knew you liked that nigga. I see you checking for him all the time. His dick must be something if it got you dressing for him."

"Shut up, bitch, you don't know my life! No, he's not going to be here!" Adrianna snapped, but she knew instantly how untrue her statement was.

She and Devynn had been a team for four years before
The Last Kings. Vinny found them, starving and hungry,
in the streets of New York. At that time, their only
means of survival was hitting a few licks and sticking
a few no-names up. The money never lasted long with
their lavish spending habits, and they were often stuck
in situations where they had to go without for days at a
time. Vinny came into their lives and saved them, and
all he asked in return was loyalty. He had to be sure he
could trust them, so he gave them a target to hit. They
had never killed anyone before, but for what he was
offering them, they would have taken anyone out of the
game. After they successfully had removed the target,
Vinny took the two of them under his wing. They moved
work underground in New York to not get the attention
of the current boss of the city at that time, but did,
however, infiltrate his cartel. Vinny needed the name of
the connect, and they got it. A short while after informing
Vinny of the name they heard, that same name appeared
in the news. The man's body was found burnt to a crisp in
his Audi. There was suspected foul play, but nothing was
ever proven. The girls didn't ever ask what happened, but
they knew then that the Italian Mafia was nothing to fuck
with. When Vinny came to them with the proposition to
be a part of maybe the biggest cartel known to the States,
they hopped at the chance, dollar signs flashing before
their hungry eyes. Their first meeting with Ray was a few
weeks before the meeting at his home.

Devynn saw immediately the spark in Adrianna's eyes
as they listened to Ray inform them of what they would
be up against. Devynn herself couldn't deny that he was
the epitome of a boss. He carried himself like he was
made of money. When he spoke, the education he
harbored was the truth. It intrigued Adrianna because
she had expected a hood nigga like the ones she'd dealt

with in the past. She knew then why Vinny invested so much in Ray. At just that first meeting with him, she had more faith in his operation then she'd had in anything for herself in her whole life.

"Mmm-hmm," was all Devynn said. Normally, she would have warned Adrianna about the decisions her heart made. But after two failed attempts at love, she hoped her girl had grown some fuckin' sense. "D and Amann coming?" she asked Adrianna instead.

"They were supposed to have been here already too," Adrianna said, the color slowly coming back to her face.

Devynn opened her mouth to speak, but just as she did, the three of them all sauntered into the club at the same time. One hell of a coincidence. Mocha walked in looking ravishing as always with her hair pulled back neatly into a ballerina bun and a skintight black dress with the sides cut out. Her face held a smug expression. She knew she was late, but she didn't care.

"Wassup?" D said once they were all at the table. "This muhfucka is popping tonight!"

"I don't give a fuck how popping it is, I'm missing out on money to be here," Amann looked at Adrianna with a look that could kill. "You think the nigga is gon' show?"

"I scoped the muhfucka out before we pulled in. I ain't see nobody suspicious," D said.

"When they ran in Taste, it was real messy," Devynn said. "They were some amateur niggas. I'm not from here, but I could tell they weren't from here either."

"You hear their voices?" Amann asked.

"Naw," Devynn shook her head. "But we need to figure out who the fuck these niggas are."

"No," Adrianna disagreed. "We need to figure out who sent them."

"The feds know what happened?" Mocha asked.

"Of course them muhfuckas know. You know somebody had to call their asses. By the time they got there
though, there weren't any bodies to be found, and they
didn't have a warrant to look around. We moved all the
money here just until the drop is made."

"You know them niggas are mad," Mocha said.

"Yea," Devynn agreed. "But until Tyler comes back, it's
best not to get on their bad side."

"Do you think they might try to hit Lace?" Mocha asked
Adrianna.

She hadn't even gotten the words out of her mouth
before Adrianna nodded her head toward the door,
reaching for her waist. Entering the strip club was a
group of men ranging in all ages, and they didn't look like
they were there to enjoy in the festivities of half-naked
bitches prancing around. Nobody but the five people
at the table noticed the newcomers, and the crowd
was so thick that it was hard to make all of them out,
but Team Mula already knew what was up. The way the
intruders moved through the crowd of people was snake-
like, and Mocha could tell by the way they were dressed
that Detroit wasn't their home. What niggas would wear
Tims to the strip club in the summertime?

"A thirsty nigga can smell a dollar from a hundred
miles away," Adrianna said, standing to her feet.

"These niggas don't know who the fuck they're fuckin'
with!" D exclaimed, infuriated, grabbing for the metal on
his hip. "How the hell they even get in?"

Before they knew what was happening, the men dispersed, covering all ground in the club and began opening
fire. At first, people thought it was a hoax, and they
cheered. But once bodies began dropping and blood
splattering in the air, the commotion began. The crowd
became a frenzy of butt-naked bitches and wannabe bal-
lers frantically trying their best to get out of the club. All

exits were covered, so no one was going anywhere. They all split up and took cover as bullets rained all around us.

"Help!"

"Oh my God!"

"I don't want to die, man!"

There were several screams being let out as more bodies dropped.

"Get down!" Amann yelled to Mocha, and he shot his pistol over her, killing two of the shooters.

Fuck this, Mocha thought. She reached and grabbed the pistol she kept strapped to her thigh and began firing too.

"There they go!" she heard somebody yell, but that didn't stop her from using her extended arm to dead them.

No mercy, she thought as she blew off the top of one of their heads close range.

Adrianna and Devynn were already on it too. Devynn had her twins out, and Mocha witnessed her pistol-whip a nigga, and then blow his brains out all over Purp and Candy. The two of them were so scared they were trembling. Before Mocha could yell for them to get to their secured entry headquarters under the club, half of Candy's head was blown off. Purp was so startled, she jumped to her feet to run, but her body soon was embedded with at least twenty rounds. Her body jerked on the ground trying to hold on to any little piece of life she had left. The four of them held their ground until their own people finally got there and swarmed the club. The gunfight seemed to last forever until the intruders finally seemed to realize that The Last Kings had them outnumbered. But by then, it was too late. They hadn't thought their plan all the way through, and it wasn't going to be over until all of them were dead. Devynn squeezed both of her triggers until they clicked empty, and when they were smoking, she was finally able to hear that there were no more shots being fired. The strobe lights just gave that effect. She stood up and looked at the bloodbath before her and saw there were at least fifty dead bodies, a few of their own laid out.

"Let's go!" D yelled to Mocha, Adrianna, Amann, and Devynn.

The parking lot outside was almost as chaotic as the scene that had just taken place in the strip club. Cars were hopping curbs just to get the fuck out of there.

"It's only a matter of time before the feds get here," Mocha said, pulling out her phone to call Ray. "Ain't no way a cleanup team can pull that shit off! It's like fifty dead muhfuckas in there!"

"I know." Amann stood back and shook his head. "We ain't got no choice but to let the shit ride."

"Sí," Adrianna said. "I have to stay since I know them fuckin' pigs are going to need to speak to me. I'm about to go and get rid of the security footage. Devynn, get Mocha home safely. Amann and D, call Ray and let him know what's up. Tell him his blocks aren't safe and neither are any of his businesses. Two in one day?"

"Something ain't right," Devynn said as they all walked quickly toward their vehicles leaving Adrianna behind.

Nobody said anything, but it was a fact that they all felt the same way.

"Today is drop-off day . . . before everything hits Amore," Devynn continued. "Those niggas had to have known that . . . but—"

"Not one nigga made a move for the money," D finished for her.

Devynn nodded her head, and Mocha shook hers.

"What were they trying to prove then?" Mocha asked, opening the door to her BMW coupe.

"The way them dudes came in execution style said it all," Amann said over his shoulder getting into his Corvette parked on the opposite side of Mocha's vehicle. "They were trying to send a message. Of what? Now, *that's* the question. I ain't recognize not one of them cats."

They all nodded, agreeing. Those men couldn't have been from Detroit. The city respected Ray too much to even dare to do that shit. But who?

"We about to go get at Ray and make this drop-off. Y'all lay low for a minute," D told us. "Dev, don't go home; go to a hotel or some shit. I'm sending ten niggas with y'all. If you need us, just call. We're going to get to the bottom of this shit."

Devynn nodded her head and hopped into the BMW with Mocha.

"Make sure Adrianna is straight too," she informed D.

"Already on it," he told her nodding to the parking lot across the street where three black Mercedes were parked almost unnoticeable in the night. "Be easy. I'll get at y'all in the morning."

And with that, he shut the door to the car. He knew Ray wasn't going to be too happy, but that was the least of his worries. His worry was that somebody had just started a war, and they had no idea why.

Chapter 17

Khiron pulled up to Amore, and he couldn't help but to be impressed with the establishment. It was nothing he'd expected. The restaurant was two stories, and the entire look of it exuded class. The parking lot was completely packed. From where he was parked, he had a clear view of the inside of the restaurant. The lower lever consisted of filled dinner tables surrounding a large dance floor with couples swaying together slowly. Everyone inside that Khiron could see was in dress attire, and he knew then that his black Armani suit was a good choice. He fixed his collar slightly before stepping out of his vehicle and making his way to the entrance.

Inside Amore, Ray was on the top level of the restaurant in the large, secluded VIP balcony section. There were five huge men that surrounded him, ready to take bullets from all sides and not letting anyone get too close. But by the look on Ray's face, nobody would be bold enough to come his way. He was infuriated with the news he'd just received. Not one but two of his businesses had been hit in one day. It couldn't have been a coincidence. He'd be a fool to think that.

"Fuck that shit. I want niggas on every block looking for the nigga that set that shit up!" Ray barked into the phone.

"A'ight, fam, but check this shit. Them niggas busted in here and never went for the money," Amann told him.

"What they want then?" Ray asked. "If it wasn't the money, what the fuck them niggas want?"

"We don't know," Amann told him.

"Find out. Drop what was at Lace off here."

"A'ight, fam."

Ray disconnected the call with Amann and waited patiently for Khiron to arrive. He was angry at what Amann had told him, but even when a war was waging, business had to continue. Ray watched as a light-skinned kid with curly hair and an impressive designer suit made his way toward where he was sitting. Before he could make it completely to the table, he was stiff-armed and stopped.

"Raise 'em," one of Ray's personal bodyguards demanded, preparing to check Khiron and strip him of any weapons.

Ray watched Khiron silently to see his reaction. The kid looked at the guards, and then at Ray.

"This is your city. I respect that. But if this Fat Albert muhfucka don't move his arm in two seconds, he won't have one to extend," the kid's voice was low but icy. "I'm here to conduct business, but I don't know you, and personally, I think it would be better if this thing stayed on my hip."

Ray chuckled, shaking his head slightly and waved at his guard to let the kid through. He motioned for Khiron to sit down, which he did, and offered him a drink, which he declined.

"You got something for me?" Ray said, cutting right to the chase.

"I wouldn't be here wasting your time if I didn't," Khiron told him.

Ray looked different from the last time he'd seen him. The last time Khiron met him, he thought he was in charge. Now he knew.

"Five minutes," Ray said.

While Khiron was busy studying him, Ray patiently gathered his thoughts. In a day's time, he found out all he needed to know about Khiron. He knew everything from where he lived all the way to which hand he wiped his ass with. He also knew that the reason Khiron was there seated in front of him in the first place was because he needed a connect. From the information Ray gathered, Atlanta was a hungry city, and Khiron was losing it. Tyler had overexaggerated the moves of the kid. Whereas he knew how to play the game, he didn't know how to own it. You could only rule with an iron fist for so long before it turned on you.

"No need for a time stamp, fam," Khiron said to Ray, leaning in on the table. "You know why I'm here. If you know why I'm here, that means you already have an answer for me."

Ray wanted to laugh at the boldness of the kid. But he didn't speak; he just stared at the young buck before him. Fear was nonexistent in his eyes as he stared back at Ray awaiting an answer. There was something about Khiron that didn't sit right with Ray, but he couldn't quite put his finger on it. They hadn't been in each other's presence but five minutes, but it was true, Ray had an answer ready for him before he even had entered his restaurant. Khiron sat before Ray young and cocky, which meant he already had two strikes against him. The only reason he decided to humor him was because he came through Tyler. But unfortunately for Khiron, the chair he sat in was as close as he would get to Ray's operation. Atlanta was a big market, but losing Khiron's business would be but a small loss. He wouldn't ever make the mistake of allowing his product to be pushed through a place if he didn't approve of the man in charge. That's how the game got fucked-up and how people got over. Ray took his time to speak, but when he did, the meaning of his words was clear.

"I would ask you how you heard about me," Ray started while pouring himself a glass of Hennessey, "but I honestly don't give a fuck. You had it right, though; this is my city." Ray raised his arms up halfway with his palms facing upward. "My establishment, my table . . . my chair," he motioned to Khiron's chair. "I'll give you a pass just because you're new in town, but had you been anyone else snapping, ya' brains would be falling from the sky like fuckin' confetti, feel me?"

Ray looked at the diamond Rolex shining on his wrist and decided to speed up the process. It was like he was holding a job interview, and he just wanted the nigga out of his office.

"You walked in here and made two mistakes. When my man says arms up, you don't speak. You do it. If he wants your guns," Ray insinuated that he knew Khiron was strapped heavy, "you drop 'em on the table. I don't like that sassy shit. That's a trait of a bitch."

Ray saw Khiron's jaw clench and unclench and a vein pulsated on his right temple, but he didn't say anything, so Ray continued.

"Understand this, my man." Ray took a gulp of his drink before staring so coldly into Khiron's eyes, Khiron felt a chill slither down his back. "My answer isn't just no. It's . . . *fuck* no. You obviously didn't know shit about me when you made contact with my right hand but let me peep you on game. You never conduct business blinded. You hopped, skipped, and took a leap of faith to my city on hope. The fuck did you think was going to happen here? You thought you were going to leave here a satisfied customer because what? What the fuck do you have to offer me? Money?" Ray scoffed.

"That's what this is about, right?" Khiron asked through clenched teeth. Bottling his anger inside was getting harder by the second. Ray's words cut into him like spikes. Nobody had ever spoken to him like that since his father was alive, and Ray wasn't his father.

"That's where you're wrong, kid," Ray shook his head at the naïvety. "Money can easily be spent, but in order for it to be made, there has to be a strong foundation. Before I make any business moves, I make it my business to know exactly who I'm dealing with. This shit is more than a sale to me. I don't give work to niggas just because they can afford it. My product will only be connected to success. Unlike you, I did my research on the man I was meeting. The little operation you have going in ya' city is too shaky to hold my shit."

Before Khiron could open his mouth to speak, he was interrupted by a hand being placed on his shoulder. He looked up and saw a middle-aged Italian man standing over but not looking at him.

"That's your cue to leave," the Italian man said in a dismissive way. "We have actual business to conduct."

He studied the man's face and felt the blood rush from his. Khiron was looking dead into the face of the man who'd ordered the hit on his father. The notorious Vinny Mancini. Anger pulsated through his veins, and his hand twitched for the gun on his waist, but when he saw one of the guards raise his eyebrow at him, he decided to chill. Instead, he stood up trying to remain professional and smirked at Ray.

"I'll be seeing you, Ray," was all he said before he made his exit. "Real soon." *Bitch nigga*, he thought walking away from the table.

He passed the entourage of Italian goons the Italian man brought with him. They all gave him looks as if to say he was beneath them. The meeting didn't go as he planned at all, but Ray was wrong. Khiron would never go somewhere without knowing about his surroundings. Khiron knew more than what he would ever let on. Ray had no idea who he was fucking with. The one thing Khiron hadn't known was that he was working with the Italians, but now that he knew, he would be sure to tread lightly.

Almost to the exit Khiron noticed a portrait hanging from one of the walls that caught his attention. It was of two women, and one he recognized right away. He was more than astonished to see Mocha hanging from the wall in front of him in the restaurant. The cream dress she wore brought out the mocha color of her skin, and the smile on her flawless face held a secret. How did she know Ray? Why was her photo in his restaurant? He guessed there were a few things about her that he didn't know. The woman standing beside her had her arm linked in Mocha's and the word *beautiful* didn't do her justice. Her long hair flowed over her shoulders and her sharp brown eyes pierced the camera. Her red lips were turned in what was supposed to be a smirk. In the picture, she wore a sophisticated form-fitting red dress, and although she faced forward, he could see her ass from the front of her. There was something familiar about the girl, but Khiron knew he'd never met her. A server was passing him, and he stopped the young Italian woman before she went by.

"Who is this?" he asked, not caring that he sounded rude. "Does she work here?"

The woman looked at him like he was crazy and laughed.

"Work here?" She shook her head. "That's Sadie. She runs this place."

Before Khiron could say another word she was gone, leaving him to stare at the picture for a few more moments.

"Sadie?" he said to himself and exited the restaurant.

There was something eating away at him while he stared at the photo. Then he remembered. She'd changed, a lot, but he could never forget her face. Fury engulfed him, and he knew he had to get out of the restaurant before he left a trail of dead bodies behind him. Enraged, he pulled out his phone and dialed out once he was safe inside his vehicle.

"What the fuck happened, Los?" he said once he heard "Hello."

"They all dead," the husky voice of one of his soldiers said.

Khiron knew that sending his men to Lace would be a suicide mission if the stories of The Last Kings preceded them. He knew it would be enough to throw Ray off of his A-game for their meeting. In the time it took Ray to pour his drink, Khiron had already scoped out the men wearing chef coats and hats going through a door that said *"Authorized Personnel Only."* That would have seemed normal . . . had it not been for the fact that he scoped out the designer pants and shoes that poked out from under the chef coats. From where Khiron had been seated, he had the perfect view of the lower level.

"But, fam, there's something else you need to know," Los said.

"What's that?"

"Ya' girl, Mocha, she was there. She's one of them, fam. She was one of the muhfuckas popping our people, nigga."

The realization hit Khiron then—hard. It was like a punch in the face. He thought he was a good liar, keeping his business dealings away from her keen nose, but Mocha, in fact, took the cake. He was hurting in his city, while that bitch was living like a fucking queen in hers. He never once questioned the designer that forever laced her body or how she could easily afford to hop on a plane to come see him whenever. When he thought about it, out of all the bitches he'd fucked with, Mocha was the only one he didn't have to give a stack of bills to go shopping. She carried herself like a bad bitch, but in all reality, she was a boss. She was a part of the expanding underground drug cartel that was obviously blossoming with the help of the Italians. He should have known the Italians were a factor when he realized Ray owned Amore. The Italians were the enemy, and Ray and the Italians were business partners. Ray was the enemy. Ray was the leader of The Last Kings. Mocha was a Last King . . . *Mocha was the enemy*. With that knowledge, Khiron also knew one other thing. He'd had the key all along; the person who would open the door to the downfall of Detroit's underground kings.

"A'ight," was all Khiron said, trying to swim through his ocean of thoughts. "What's going on now?"

"They moved it," Los said, referring to the money that had been at Lace.

"Where?" he asked, but before he got an answer, he watched a Corvette pull up to the valet parking of the restaurant.

Two men exited the vehicle, each holding a fat suitcase, and Khiron couldn't help the smile coming to his face. He disconnected the call and gave himself a silent praise. Way before Khiron made his trip into Detroit, he sent a handful of niggas before him to watch the movements of Ray's operation. After a few weeks of surveillance, Khiron had to admit that Ray was smooth. His operation was flawless, and he'd never seen another like it. The Last Kings was a force not many could fuck with, but still, the men Khiron sent were able to figure out when the drop-off days and times were. The point of the run-ins that he'd formulated wasn't ever to rob Ray at that time. He knew Ray ran a handful of businesses and hitting them all would be too much work. But what Khiron did know was that with the thought of potentially getting robbed came a sense of security. Ray would want all of his money on lockdown and in one place. Seeing the Corvette pull up, Khiron knew his theory had been correct. The theory being that Ray would move all of the money to the safest place he could think of until it was ready to be placed. As a hustler himself, he knew how risky depositing large amounts of drug money in the bank was. Ray needed to clean it first. Khiron's original plan was to conduct business and obtain a connect . . . while robbing him blind. But after the way Ray spoke to him and seeing the portrait in the restaurant, his plans had changed. A sick smile came to his face. He wasn't going to rob Ray of the money sitting inside of Amore, but now he knew where the heart of the whole operation was located.

It was no longer business; it was personal. Khiron was going to kill each and every one of those Italians. Since Vinny's bullet was the one that pierced his father's skull, he would get it the worst. Khiron's blood raged when he thought about how that piece of shit had touched him. Only one word pumped through his brain. *Revenge.* He picked up his phone and called Mocha.

"Hello?" she answered. Her voice sounded exhausted.

"What up, bae, where you at?" Khiron asked, trying his best to keep the disgust from his voice.

"Nothing, just watching some TV." Khiron shook his head at how easily the lie rolled off her tongue.

"My plane just touched down," he lied. "Meet me at my hotel in a few hours."

He heard her sit up straight through the phone.

"You're *here?*" He heard a mixture of concern and excitement in her voice.

"Yea, bae, I wanted to surprise you," he lied again. "I tied up a few loose ends in the A and thought it was time for a little venture into my wifey's city. See how she's living."

His last words had an icy effect to them, but Mocha barely took notice.

"OK, um, text me what hotel and the room number. I have some shit to handle right now but a few hours sounds like a plan." Her voice dropped as if she didn't want anyone around her to hear the plans she was making.

"A'ight, ma, I'ma see you," and with that, Khiron disconnected the call.

His eyes stayed on the Corvette until the two men returned to the vehicle. They didn't know it, but that night would be their last night on earth alive. It was true that Detroit was Ray's city, and he ran it out of love instead of fear, but it was Khiron's game, and when he was done with The Last Kings, his name would shake the bravest of hearts. He was going to wreak havoc and torture them all. He'd vowed long ago that his father's death wouldn't be in vain. The shit at Lace and the hair salon was nothing compared to what he had in store for all them muhfuckas. When he saw the car prepare to pull off, he made one last phone call and began to tail behind it.

"Let the war begin."

Chapter 18

"What was that about?" Vinny asked Ray once the two shook hands.

Ray leaned back in his seat and smirked. "Business as usual," he shrugged. "Little niggas always approaching for work but can't even deliver."

Vinny stared at the man before him and chuckled at his suave. Ray was no longer the kid with potential he'd met with in the backseat of a Mercedes. He knew that investing in Ray would be good for business, but in all actuality, Ray had invested in him. Vinny was in awe at the way Ray had branched off of him. Ray was the connect to six major drug-demanding cities, so, in turn, Vinny was all of their connect. The drug demand was so high that if Vinny didn't want to conduct business with anyone *but* Ray, he would never have to. The Italian drug cartel was making millions off of one operation, and that was why, in Vinny's eyes, Ray had rightfully earned the title of a king.

Ray asked Vinny to have a seat, but he declined.

"Business as usual," he said, but in so many words, he was telling Ray that he was just there to pick up and get out.

"A'ight," Ray said nodding his head. "It's all here. Miami, DC, LA, Chicago, Houston, and New York. Two mil."

Vinny raised his eyebrow at Ray's carelessness, but didn't say anything. He trusted Ray's judgment, and he also knew that Amore was the safest place for the money. He nodded to his men to go grab it and shook Ray's hand once more before he too made his exit. That was the way Vinny was; he was never in one spot for more than twenty minutes. He also never went anywhere without an army of Italians behind him and an automatic pistol.

Ray rubbed his facial hair and looked at the phone sitting on the table. He had no doubt in his mind that his generals would handle the little situation that took place that night, but when it came down to it, he knew he needed both his left and right hand. Something told him that the fuckery would continue, and that somebody was sending him a message. Ray was low-key glad that his two leading generals would be touching down in the morning; the horrendous scent of an upcoming war was frozen at the tip of his nose.

Chapter 19

After that night in the restaurant, things between Tyler and I were a little awkward, but we tried to make the best of our arrangement. We went on many tours and ventured off a lot by ourselves. No matter how hard I tried, I couldn't bring myself to be evil to him, although he'd broken my heart twice. I didn't know if it was love or the simple fact that I respected his loyalty to the game. He was right, after all. Mixing business with pleasure never worked, and I knew the life span of a hustler was short. Instead of indulging in the negatives, I decided to shoot for positives with Tyler. He surprised me our last night in the beautiful place and something in the air changed between us.

"You can't just tell me what it is?" I asked him, pouting as I tried to keep my balance on the sand.

"Then it wouldn't be called a 'surprise,' ma," Tyler smiled at me and grabbed ahold of my waist, assisting me with walking.

"Well, you could have at least told me we were going to the beach," I cut my eyes at him holding his arm lightly. "I wouldn't have put the fuckin' Red Bottoms on. My shoes are going to be ruined!"

"Chill, Say, plus, you have about a hundred more pairs where those came from," he laughed.

Before I could say anything else smart, we came up on the most beautiful beach scene I'd ever seen in my life. It was like a movie. On the beach, overlooking the water, a single table with a white tablecloth and two chairs was set up. On the table were two plates with covers over them, two wineglasses, and a candle in the center. Around the table, rose petals were scattered and a piano—yes, a fucking piano—played soft tunes into the night.

"Tyler," I said breathlessly and stopped in my tracks. "Is all that . . .?"

"For you?" He stood in front of me and grabbed my hands. "Yes. It's our last night in paradise, and I wanted to do something special for you, ma."

"Like an apology?" I pressed my luck.

"Real niggas," he said, "don't apologize. But they do make up for their wrongs."

"Like an apology," I said matter-of-factly, and he laughed.

"Shut up and come on." He urged me toward the table.

He pulled my chair out for me, and when I sat, he pushed me back in. When he joined me on the opposite side of the table, he wore a huge Kool-Aid smile.

"What?" I asked, feeling myself blush at the way he was looking at me.

"You look gorgeous," was all he said.

I rolled my eyes, not wanting to get the wrong idea again.

"Hungry?"

"Hell yea," I said and felt my stomach growl. "What's on the menu?"

"Oh, nothing," Tyler said smugly, lifting both of our tops off of our plates. "Just some macaroni and cheese, fried chicken, black-eyed peas, and corn bread."

The aroma filled my nostrils, and I was in heaven. The sight of the food made my mouth water. It looked absolutely scrumptious!

"My favorite!" I exclaimed in shock. "How'd you know?"

After the question was out, I realized how dumb it sounded. Tyler probably knew me as well as Ray did. It didn't hit me until then that I barely knew anything personal about the man I thought I loved.

"It's not as good as Grandma Rae's, but I tried," he shrugged.

It touched me that he'd gone to such great lengths to make my last night there paradise, but then I had to stop myself before I got to thinking too much.

This is why Ray sent him; he's just doing his job, I told myself.

"Thank you," I said and dug into my plate not able to stop.

He was right, it was nothing like Grandma Rae's, but it was still delicious. We ate until our stomachs were full, and I could see a little bulge in my Dolce dress.

"I didn't know you could cook," I told him, wiping my mouth on a napkin.

"There's a lot you don't know about me, ma," he said and pushed his empty plate away from him. "When I was young, my mom was always gone. So I had to learn to take care of home myself."

I nodded my head, knowing how that was. I could see why he and Ray were best friends.

"Tell me about yourself, Tyler. There's a lot I don't know, but I would like to," I told him in all honesty.

"There's not enough time in the world for my story, Say," he chuckled. "Just know we all got a story, and right now, mine is here. With you."

"Make time then," I said, not wanting to let him off that easy.

I knew that was probably the only time I'd get him alone again. Once we got back to Detroit, it would be all business and no play once again. The Sadie in Jamaica and the Sadie in Detroit were two separate people, and I knew the same held true for Tyler. I wanted to get the most out of it. Since the incident at the restaurant, no longer did my clit throb for Tyler's presence, but when he was away, I still did miss him. I didn't want to go back to Detroit and it still be the same way, because he'd be away a lot longer than thirty minutes there. If I couldn't have him as my man, lover, or whatever, I would settle for whatever piece of him he would give. When I said I wanted to know him, I meant it. Tyler looked at me, confusion on his face.

"I promise I won't ever make any type of advance on you again," I said, placing my chair directly on the right of his and sitting in it. "This is our last night here, so if I'm not going to get any dick, you have to give me something." I shrugged, placing my elbow on the table and placing my head in my hand. I'd kept it one hundred with him, and I was expecting the same in return. He studied my face intently to see if I was serious.

"A'ight, ma, since you insist. What do you wanna know?" he asked.

"Everything," I stated simply, and he paused again.

"Here's the shortened version. I was born in Detroit and raised by a mother who worked three jobs just to keep a roof over my head. My old man was an abusive alcoholic, but once I turned fifteen, all that shit stopped. I almost killed that nigga after he beat my moms so bad she had a broken jaw and rib cage." He stopped, but I didn't interrupt. I wanted him to continue. "I started hustling at eighteen with Ray, just getting it how we lived. I came up, fast. We always had a business plan. The Last Kings started with us. I don't know if he ever told you that, but this shit popped off long before Coopa ran the city. Shit was coo for a while. My mom only had to work one job since I was taking care of the bills and shit. Everything was going good until some hating-ass niggas got wind of our money chase and did a drive-by on our house. Unfortunately, for them, I wasn't there, but unfortunately for me, my moms was. She was in the middle of cooking dinner when the shots hit her body. My little sister was upstairs in her bed asleep. Didn't even know what happened."

"Tyler, I'm so sorry," I said, sitting up straight. "I didn't know."

"It's good, shorty." Tyler shook his head, the look in his eyes distant. "I found out who did it and sent all their body parts to their mothers in little freezer bags."

I'd forgotten the illusion that Jamaica had given me of Tyler, and it was false. It was true that he could be sweet, but that's because we were on the same team. At heart, Tyler was a cold-blooded killer. It came with the job description. Mercy wasn't even a word to him. It didn't exist.

"How is Marie by the way?" I asked, knowing he kept his little sister's whereabouts low-key. I knew she had to be about eighteen now though.

"Good," Tyler smiled at the thought of his little sister. "A lot like you actually."

"That's not a good thing," I smiled.

"Who says?" Tyler held my gaze deeply, and I had to avert his gaze.

"Have you ever been in love, Tyler?" I asked the sand.

"I've had my share of women, but, no, I can't say I've ever loved one of 'em. In the life I'm living, there honestly isn't enough time for it."

I nodded at his answer, slightly relieved that no woman had ever captured his heart.

"What about you?" he asked, catching me off guard.

"Have I ever been in love?" I repeated the question and thought about the pain I'd suffered as a young teenager with my mother's devil. "No, I've never let a man get that close to me. I've never even allowed myself to have a real boyfriend. Bosses don't have time for pain."

I answered the question, trying not to think about my past trauma, but the sound of my own screams invaded my mind, and I couldn't stop the tears from flowing. I removed myself from the table and went to stand by the piano facing the water. Gasping for air, I tried to calm myself down. Through my long wet eyelashes I could barely see the moon reflecting off of the water. Tyler's presence was soon felt behind me, and I tried to stop the tears that kept coming. Nobody but Mocha had ever seen me cry.

"Sadie, what's wrong, ma?" Tyler asked grabbing my shoulders and pulling me to him, but I couldn't speak.

That one question sent me diving deep into the memories I'd tried so hard to erase. All I could see was Nino's face as he mounted me and took the only thing I'd ever had to offer. Nino was the reason I bled every time when I first started having sex on my own free will. Nino was the reason why I'd never trusted any man besides Ray. Nino was the reason why my feelings for Tyler were so jumbled. How could I love a man when I had no idea what love was? How could any man love a woman like me? I had too much baggage, and that was why whenever any relationship of mine seemed to be blooming, I did something on purpose to end it. Ending any connection between me and that person . . . It was the only thing I could control. That way, I didn't feel the pain. But right there on that beach? I felt it. I felt it all.

"Tyler, just let me go!" I yelled, trying to fight him off as a sea of emotions swarmed over me.

But he didn't. We fell into the sand, and he held me through every sob, stroking my hair and telling me it would be all right. Whatever it was, it would be all right.

When I was finally done, I wiped my eyes and turned to face him.

"I'm so sorry," I told him, and he cupped my face in his hands. "I didn't mean to ruin another dinner."

"It's coo, ma." Concern drenched his face. "What's going on?"

I studied him. A real nigga, a dying breed. In that split second, I knew I could trust him. I told him everything—about the rapes, how I was forced to hustle, and how I came to stay with Grandma Rae. He never once interrupted me. When I told him about the rapes, I'd never seen him look so mad before. The vein on his temple pulsated violently, and when I was done, I begged him not to tell Ray. I couldn't bear the thought of Ray knowing about the skeletons in my closet. He promised me and held me again.

"If that nigga wasn't already dead, I'd send an army of niggas to blow every one of his fuckin' limbs off, ma," he said into my hair. "I swear on my life, no man will ever hurt you again. They're going have to get through me first. You hear me?"

He lifted my chin with his finger, and I looked deep into his eyes. I could see that not only did my story make him angry, but there was pain there too. He hurt because I hurt. Something deep inside me erupted, and I knew then, at that moment, that my feelings for that man weren't faux. I nodded my head because I believed him with every fiber of my being.

"I love you, Tyler," I was able to breathe just before he kissed me.

Chapter 20

Devynn was livid as she waited a little after two o'clock for Tyler and Sadie to emerge from the large crowd of people exiting the airport. She leaned on her newly washed red Audi, barely able to keep her balance. Anger coursed through her, but the pain she felt almost knocked her off of her feet. Although in a pair of shorts and boyfriend T-shirt, she was still hot, and patience was running low. When she finally spotted their smiling faces, the look she wore instantly wiped their smiles from existence. There was a different glow on Sadie's normally serious face, but she didn't acknowledge it when they approached her. She had news to tell them that would ground them, but she knew that the airport was not the place to reveal such news. She also knew that Tyler had something like a temper, and all the people exiting the airport to meet loved ones one minute might be laid out on the ground dead the next.

Tyler wasn't a dumb nigga; he knew instantly something was up. There was a sadness so powerful in Devynn's eyes he knew something horrible had happened. Devynn was the type of bitch that never showed emotion; she was taught to be hardened to the core.

"Even in the worst pain of your life, never show a nigga that you feel *anything*," was something she was known for saying.

Tyler and Sadie exchanged glances, but Tyler waited until they pulled off from the airport to say anything.

"What's up?" he asked her looking at her from the passenger seat.

Devynn took a breath before she spoke. "While you two have been enjoying ya' fun in the sun and shit," she started, her voice wavering slightly, "muhfuckas been here wilding off their asses. They hit Lace and the salon."

Sadie leaned toward the front from the backseat. Devynn recapped the story for the two of them since they were the only ones MIA. Sadie was hot. It read all over her face.

"Why didn't Ray call me?" she fumed. "I would have been here!"

"Chill, Sadie," Tyler tried to calm her. He studied the way Devynn gripped the steering wheel as she drove on the highway, and he knew there was more to the story that she hadn't said yet. "What's going on now, Dev? They get the people that did the shit, 'cause if not, on God, I'ma handle that."

Devynn shook her head and gripped the steering wheel even harder. They couldn't see but tears were forming in her eyes.

"Now . . ." she started but choked up, letting tears that had been nonexistent for five years roll down her face.

"Talk, nigga!" Tyler barked at her.

"Amann and D are dead!" Devynn yelled, pulling over on the highway. She got out and slammed her door. "Fuuuck!" she screamed at the onlooking cars and put her hands on her naturally curly Afro.

A look of shock was frozen on both Tyler and Sadie's faces, but soon Tyler's brow furrowed, and rage in his whole body language was visible. His bros couldn't be dead. Nah, not Amann and D. Those dudes were survivors, real soldiers. The Last Kings was created before them, but could never be the same after them. Never. He and Sadie both hopped out after Devynn and went to stand before her as she screamed. Tyler reached out and snatched the sunglasses off of her face before gripping her shoulders. He needed to see the lie in them, but when he didn't, he let her go, rubbing his chin and shaking his head.

"Nah." He couldn't believe it.

They had all come from different backgrounds, but the operation had pulled them all close-knit together. They all had each other's backs. Or that's how it was supposed to be.

"They're dead," Devynn said through clenched teeth. "As in hearts stopped. As in their bodies were found in D's Corvette this morning. And, Ty, yo, their fucking heads were strapped in car seats *behind 'em!* These niggas are fuckin' sick, yo!"

Sadie went to Devynn and held her as she sobbed. Just like Tyler had done her.

"Whoever did it carved some shit on their chests. It said, *'None of you or yours are safe.'* Amann saved my life, Say! If it wasn't for that nigga, I'd be dead grass, and now look at him!" Devynn couldn't control her rogue emotions.

Tyler stood anguished, watching the women cling to each other. The Last Kings didn't start shit with nobody; the money was the only motive. Tyler knew the game. The deaths of D and Amann meant that someone had just started a war, and so far, they were losing. Whoever had ordered the hits was like a phantom, or at least that's what he got from Devynn's story. He knew it was something to worry about if Ray had no clue who the fuck was behind the madness. What he did know, though, was that the message was loud and clear. The nigga was coming at their necks. Now that they knew to watch their backs, it would be hard to catch them slipping again. There was only one person on his mind, and although no one knew her whereabouts but him, he knew to never underestimate his enemy.

"Get me to my car, Dev," he ordered. "Get Say to Ray's, and I'ma be there later. I gotta go get Marie."

Chapter 21

Tyler pulled into the apartment complex that he had set his sister up in. It was in a nice community shielded by a neighborhood of houses in the suburbs. He liked it because in order to get to it, you had to know exactly where you were going. Tyler knocked on the apartment door on the first floor that was hers and waited for her to open it.

"Come in!" the soft voice of a woman said from the other side.

Tyler entered the apartment with a grim look on his face. A beautiful, skinny, young woman was perched on a leather couch wearing silk Gucci pajamas smiling at him. She too was light-skinned with soft, short, curly hair and hazel eyes. Her cheekbones were high, and her nose sharp. She was the female version of Tyler.

"What I tell you about locking that door?" he said as his greeting to his baby sister.

"Well, hello to you too, nigga." She extended a wary eye. "What are you doing here anyway? I'd think you'd be resting after your little vacation."

She asked that like Tyler didn't stop by frequently just to make sure she was straight. But he always called before he just showed up. Something was up, she could tell by the look in his eye. She could read her brother like a book.

"Put some clothes on; we gotta go," he said simply like her whole life wasn't inside of that large one-bedroom apartment. To him, though, all of that shit was replaceable; her life wasn't. "Grab what you need and meet me in the car."

Marie wanted to protest, but she knew better. Even if she did, she saw the livid expression on her big brother's face and knew her words wouldn't do much of anything but stall time. She'd just gotten settled into her apartment and all she wanted to do was enjoy peace in her own area. Tyler planned on moving Marie into Ray's estate until things blew over and until they knew who was starting a war with them. There would be security and watchful eyes day and night. He couldn't bear the thought of losing his baby sister like he lost his mother. He'd been good about separating his street life and his relationship with his sister. He took her out of the hood just so she wouldn't be subjected to that life. He vowed to do any and everything to protect the small piece he had left of his family. Marie was a strong woman, and although she'd never toted a gun, stared into the eyes of a dying man, or touched a kilo of cocaine, she understood the game. Wherever she went, she was treated like a princess just because of who her brother was and who he was affiliated with. In every department store, she was waited on hand and foot. She had her own car, but Tyler insisted on her being chauffeured around in a bulletproof limousine if she ever needed to go anywhere. Her face was rarely seen on the streets, but when it was, Tyler made sure she always wore a smile.

Marie stood up to get dressed but came to an abrupt stop at the sound of several cars screeching to a halt outside of her living-room window. Running to the window, Tyler glanced out and saw several men dressed casually hop out of three black Jeeps, guns drawn. Marie saw them too and a look of terror crossed her face. Tyler cursed himself because he and Ray were the only ones who knew of her whereabouts, which meant he must have been followed.

"Ty," Marie whispered behind him.

"Be easy, sis." He turned to her, knowing they didn't have much time. "Take this, we getting out of this bitch."

He handed her a 9-mm pistol, glad he'd taught her how to use it, though he hoped she'd never have to. Several shots rang out, and the two dropped to the floor in sync, but no bullets came into the apartment. Ray found out what they had lit up when he looked back outside of the window. His Mercedes sat on four flats, all the windows were shot out, and the hood of the car was a blaze of fire. He saw the men taking cover just in time to grab Marie and run to the front door. Behind them, the explosion of the car was so powerful, the living-room windows shattered, and Ray shielded Marie's body from the glass and debris.

"Come on!" he ordered.

He exited the apartment first, gun raised. When he saw nobody in the hallway, he took Marie by the hand and ran toward the staircase in the back of the apartment. He'd cased the apartment before he moved Marie into it so he knew there was a window on the third floor that overlooked the swimming pool of the complex. It was their only bet, especially since he knew exit doors were out of the question. He knew the building was probably surrounded. Marie tried her best to keep up, knowing that if she so much as stumbled, they were dead. Behind her, she heard a door open just as they turned to rush up the first flight of stairs and out of sight. Her heart pounded violently in her chest and feet moved faster than they ever had before. She knew that if her brother was running, something bad was going down.

"They ain't in here! Raid this muhfucka!" a deep voice echoed throughout the apartment building. "That was Tyler's car in the parking lot. They're here somewhere."

"Tyler, where are we going?" Marie panted to her brother as they ran up the third flight of stairs.

He ignored her and continued running as fast as his Retro Laker 6s would take him, never once letting go of her hand. If it had just been him alone in the apartment, he would have gone out blazing with the niggas, but his brotherly love kicked in. Keeping Marie safe was his only purpose at that point in time. Finally, they reached the window on the third floor, and Ray shot it out.

"We have to jump," he told her, tucking his gun away and picking her up like a baby. He kissed her on the cheek. "Don't be scared," he whispered into her ear after seeing her eyes widen in fright.

He stepped up and jumped just as the footsteps coming up the stairs after them got closer. Marie cringed and gripped Tyler's neck as they dropped from the third floor toward the pool. Marie gasped for air just before the water hit her body. The impact of the water was more than just painful, but Tyler refused to let go of his sister. They sank toward the bottom of the pool briefly, but the presence of bullets hitting the water forced power into Tyler's long legs, and he kicked his hardest until they surfaced. Around him he saw that the water no longer was clear, but stained red as innocent bystanders trying to enjoy a day at the pool became helpless victims in a manhunt. They acted as shields for Ray and Marie when they exited the pool in a coughing frenzy.

"G-go!" Tyler coughed at Marie once they'd emerged from the pool with drenched and heavy clothes.

The pool area was chaotic with people screaming frantically, pushing each other, trying to get through the exit gate. Tyler and Marie ducked and dodged bullets but saw many people drop dead around them. A woman Marie recognized and her infant son lay dead and bloody in a pool chair, but Marie focused on the purse that lay next to her. She made a quick dash to the purse and snatched it up. It was her turn to lead Ray.

"This way! She never parked in the parking lot!" Marie yelled back at Tyler, pushing through the crowd trying to get through.

The sight of the gun in her hand made people scatter, clearing a way for her and Tyler to run through. Marie rummaged through the woman's purse until she found a cell phone, the garage door opener, and car keys. She then tossed the purse onto the ground and led Tyler to the garage that matched the number on the garage door opener. She'd pressed the button way before they got there, and they wasted no time hopping in the beat-up Toyota Camry. Their clothes soaked the cloth interior, and Tyler reversed like a madman out of the garage. He sped the opposite way out of the complex, glad the car at least had tinted windows. In order to exit the complex completely, he had to double back around and pass the parking lot, which was nothing but a sight of fire and smoke due to Tyler's still burning Mercedes. His eyes zoomed in on the Jeeps the men had hopped out of and focused on the personalized license plates. Personalized license plates meant that the vehicles weren't rentals. *Atlanta* read clear as day. They were from Atlanta. Ray had just denied the city's boss business with The Last Kings.

"Damn," Tyler said, whipping out of the complex and through the suburban neighborhood.

He knew who was behind the bloodshed in the city. What was even more fucked-up was that he was the one who'd welcomed him into Detroit by even responding to his phone call. He reached into his pocket for his phone, but realized upon looking at the water damaged device, it was of no use.

"Hand me that phone, Marie," he said taking his eyes off the road as they passed an intersection in the neighborhood. He had to call Ray ASAP and let his boy know what was good.

To the right of him, he saw that traffic had a stop sign, but he saw too late that the big black truck headed straight for them had no intentions of stopping. Before they knew what had hit them, Marie's side of the car was violently rammed, causing Tyler to lose control of the vehicle. Marie's screams were deafening, and Tyler tried and failed to regain control of the car. They spun out until they finally crashed into a tree. Marie's head had hit the dashboard, so there was blood trickling down her face, and Ray was pinned to the steering wheel. He tried to reach his gun when he saw the group of men running toward the vehicle, but it was no use.

"Marie," he said to his sister whose tears were mixing into the blood streaming down her cheeks. "No!"

Her window was busted out and a hand grabbed her by her short hair, yanking her through the window.

"No! No!" she tried to fight, wriggling her body and kicking her feet, but they were too strong for her.

"Contain that bitch!" a voice said, but she couldn't focus on the face.

Her vision was getting blurry, the trauma of her head injury was causing her to blackout. The last thing she saw while she was being carried swiftly away to the big black truck was a gun being aimed at her brother's head. One last tear dropped from her eye, and she blacked out, but not before she heard the bullet that ended her brother's life.

Chapter 22

Khiron sat on the large king-sized bed inside the room of his penthouse suite watching Mocha move her body seductively before him. The lights were dim. She turned around, exposing the way her ass ate up her thong just before she began making it clap. No music played; she rocked to her own beat. All she wanted to do was please her man and forget about all of the chaos in her life. With Amann and D's double funeral the next day, she needed something to drown out the pain of losing two men she'd come to think of as her brothers. It was her second night with Khiron, and she noticed he'd been real distant, but she knew a little of her loving would bring him back to her.

Khiron was toying with Mocha, playing her like a game of chess. He just needed his next move to be his best move. Manipulation was the game, and he needed it to be in his favor. He wanted nothing more than to put a bullet in her head, but what use would her corpse be to him? Her smooth mocha skin and plump ass enticed him, and he felt his manhood grow three more inches. Khiron couldn't lie. He loved Mocha. Women, of course, caught his attention in the past, but no one but she was able to catch his heart. That made the betrayal he felt all the more wrong. It caused him some grief to know that she would have to die with the rest of her team. He had a small army of niggas just waiting for the word, but the thing was, Mocha hadn't given him anything.

He sighed and shook his head. He had to speed up the process. His operation couldn't wait for him to get his nut off. He needed to formulate a plan before Ray traced the deaths of the two men he killed back to him. Khiron was ruthless in the head. He felt nothing when he cut off their heads with the sharpened machete. It was refreshing to him. All of them would die gruesome deaths, and when he got to the Italians, he would do the same to them. He was crazy as hell for going at the Italian cartel, but he knew killing The Last Kings one by one would send them a message. Nino's legacy was not to be fucked with.

"Bring that ass here," he bit his lip at her, and she smiled, sashaying his way.

"Mmm, you ready for me already?" Mocha said seductively, straddling him.

"Naw, chill, ma." Khiron placed his hands on her waist, stopping her from grinding on him. He knew he wouldn't be able to stop her once she got going. "I just wanna kick something to you right quick."

Mocha cocked her head at him and eyed him with her light brown eyes, curious as to what he had to say.

"Well, speak, nigga," she told him. "This pussy can't wait all day."

Khiron thought quickly about his plan, knowing that everything about it was pointing against him, but putting Mocha in the know was the only way she would sing information. If it didn't work, it would be nothing to just put her to sleep forever in that hotel suite.

"I know about you, ma," Khiron started and immediately saw the look on her face go from pleasure to nervous.

"Know about me?" she giggled, trying to catch herself. "I would hope you knew me. You've been fuckin' with me for a while now, bae. Now, come on and make me feel good."

"Naw, Mocha," Khiron pushed her hands off of him. "You know what I mean. *The Last Kings* ring a bell?"

Mocha's face paled, and she stood to her feet.

"Were you ever going to tell me?" he asked her, seriously wanting that answer.

"No." Mocha didn't even have to think before she answered, and that made Khiron even angrier than when he got wind of who she really was.

Mocha saw the anger in Khiron's face and couldn't help not giving a damn. She didn't feel that Khiron needed to know about her business dealings. It wasn't any of his business. She also didn't inform him of her affiliation in fear that he would try to use her connections for his own personal gain. Now, she felt something in the air change between them, and she didn't like or trust it. She knew about Khiron. She wouldn't have kept visiting him in Atlanta if she didn't do some kind of research. His body count stretched a long way. He'd killed mercilessly to obtain his spot as Atlanta's boss, so she knew that he was nobody you wanted to go toe to toe with. Khiron just nodded his head.

"I met with Ray a few nights ago." Khiron's intentions were no longer to keep his words sweet. He wanted to cut her deep—to the core. "That nigga, he's a true boss. I'm not going hate on 'em. But every boss gets caught slipping, right?"

Mocha stopped dressing herself and stared at Khiron in only a pair of shorts and her bra. The mood had been killed for her, and her mind-set was changing from girlfriend Mocha to Last Kings Mocha. The man before her was not the man she loved. The look in his eyes held something completely different now. It was the look of a hungry dog.

"The fuck are you talking about, Khiron? The Last Kings don't get caught slipping, least of all Ray, so quiet that noise."

Khiron stood up and walked slowly to the nightstand beside his bed. From it, he pulled out a machete. The same machete he used to kill D and Amann, in fact. It still was stained with their dried-up blood.

"I'm assuming that's what those other two niggas thought. Right?" He smirked at Mocha, and her mouth dropped.

"Y-you?" Mocha's mind reeled looking at the weapon. "You killed my brothers?"

Khiron's connect was just sent to prison, and he just said he had a meeting with Ray. She remembered Adrianna mentioning something about a meeting with someone from Atlanta that he turned away. Mocha didn't really pay her any mind since Ray had a lot of business meetings. Standing there, she wished she'd paid more attention and didn't leave her gun in the car. She backed up as far as she could until her back was pressed up against the wall, and Khiron advanced on her.

"What do you want, Khiron?" she asked him. "Why did you kill them?"

"I want it all," he smiled, knowing his answer answered both questions. "I'm going to kill anyone in the way of what's mine."

In Khiron's crazy way of thinking, Ray's operation was rightfully his since it was given to him by his father's killers.

"No!" Mocha cried out. "You bitch! You didn't come here to see me . . . You're trying to take the city; *our* city."

"Yea," Khiron shrugged. "Pretty much . . . and you're going to help."

"Fuck you." Mocha tried to make a dash for the door, but Khiron grabbed her forcefully by her neck.

Mocha was a fighter, but her punches did nothing to Khiron's big build. Her energy was fading, along with her breath so she stopped fighting after a few seconds. Khiron pinned her back up against the wall, but as he opened his mouth to speak, his phone vibrated with a message. Knowing what it was about, he glanced at it, smiled, and turned his attention back to the woman he was suffocating.

"I don't want to kill you, Mocha, but I swear to God, I will." His voice was like venom, and Mocha's body was paralyzed.

She felt hot tears coming to her eyes as she gulped for air and stared into the cold eyes of the man she once loved and now felt nothing but hatred for. She saw her life flash before her eyes when his grip around her neck tightened, and then loosened.

"I know you, Mocha. You're not a hustler, and you're not a killer. You kind of just fell into this profession, and I want to take you out. Your place is beside the man in charge." Khiron decided to change up his approach. "I'm so sorry, babe. I don't want to hurt you. You know I love you, ma, but this is business. A woman of your caliber shouldn't have to work . . . ever. Help me, ma. I promise I got you."

Mocha's mind was reeling. Her loyalty was to The Last Kings, and a part of her wanted to spit in his face for what he was implying she do. But another part of her had to admit that he was right. The cartel was, and had always been, Sadie's idea; Mocha was just ride or die. But now, faced with the presence of death, she knew she wasn't ready to perish. The lavish life she lived came with a price, and with every heart her bullets pierced, a piece of her soul left her body. She felt like a traitor. She had said she would go to the grave for her team. The tattoo branded on her body made that promise . . . but promises were meant to be broken. After the deaths of D and Amann, the pain she felt was unbearable, and feeling the tears trailing down her face, she knew The Last Kings would never be the same. She knew she only had seconds to make her decision . . . So she did.

"Just promise me one something." Mocha choked on her tears and closed her light brown eyes. "And I'll do whatever you want."

Khiron felt the sticky smile forming slowly on his face. "Name it, ma." He wiped the tears from her face like he wasn't the one causing them.

"Sadie lives." Mocha's eyes shot open, and there was a fire so strong in them, Khiron almost took a step back.

He studied her, knowing that if he said no, he would have to kill her and find another way of getting to Ray in a day's time. But he also knew that what she was asking for was a promise that he couldn't keep. Still, he looked into her eyes and put on the most sincere face he could muster.

"You have my word, ma." The lie burned on his tongue, and he cupped her face. "I promise."

Chapter 23

Ray stood in an all-black suit watching Adrianna say her last good-byes to Amann and D once they were in the earth. Sadie, Devynn, and Mocha already said theirs and were in the backseat of the limousine that was waiting to take them all back to Ray's home. Although covered by a black lace veil, he could still read the sadness drenched on Adrianna's face. She wore a black Versace dress that stopped just below her knees and a pair of all-black open-toe Christian Louboutin four-inch heels. Her lips, stained with lipstick the color of red wine, were pursed as she dropped the roses on their tombstones right beside each other. The deaths of two of their own hadn't really set in until she saw them lying lifeless in their coffins. The coroner had done a good job. He'd made them look as if they were asleep. Buried like two bosses. They were in tuxedos, and the collars covered their severed necks. The two of them came in the game together, so it was only right for them to leave the same way . . . just not like that. The way they were murdered was malicious intent and with no reasoning. She could have seen if they had started a war with another territory, but truth was, they were too busy making money to pay attention to the moves of the other cities unless they were on the come up. She knew it couldn't have been either of the six they had business with. But who?

"Whoever did this," Adrianna spoke when she felt Ray creep up behind her, "will burn. I put that on my life."

Ray nodded his head in agreement. Adrianna turned to Ray and looked at him through the veil on her face.

"They didn't deserve this!" she exclaimed, tears forming in her eyes. "They were just supposed to be dropping off the money and coming back to meet us! When they didn't call, I didn't trip because I thought they were with you and—I should have called or something. Fuck! How did this happen?"

Nothing hurt a leader more than losing his own to the unknown. Since the day Ray found out about their deaths, he had his people on every block looking for anything that seemed even *slightly* out of place. So far nothing. It was pissing him off to the point of no return that nobody had any info. He'd even contacted a few people in other cities, high and low, to see if anyone had any wind of a hit going down in Detroit. Nobody knew anything. He knew he had to grab the situation by its reins before Vinny thought he was losing control of the city. Ray ran the city with power but also with love, and it showed him love back. He knew that it couldn't have been anyone there who killed D or Amann.

"I got niggas on every block looking for unfamiliar faces, ma," Ray told her. "I'm trying."

"Not hard enough!" she barked, her accent thick. "Their blood should be streaming through the streets of the fuckin' city, just like our brothers'!"

"I can't dead a fuckin' ghost, Adrianna!" Ray yelled back.

He had never raised his voice at a woman, but the truth was, the fact that he had no leads and no idea of who committed the murders was eating away at him. He was supposed to be in tune with every happening in his city, but somebody got him. He knew that whoever did it was bold, but not bold enough to come at him directly. Instead, they went an even smarter route. Most niggas would want you to know the damage they caused, but whoever it was wanted Ray to be in a distraught position. He knew that much because it was what he would do, and knowing that, he knew he needed to clear his mind. Adrianna looked slightly taken aback, and Ray instantly felt guilty.

"My bad, ma," he said.

Adrianna and Ray never crossed the boundaries between business and work; but it couldn't be denied that there was a spark. He had a soft spot for her, and over the time of The Last Kings' takeover, it had often been tempting to make her wifey. She was everything he needed in a woman, nothing like the women he one-nighted and sent on their way. She was the type of woman that would be a forever thing. But he knew it couldn't happen; just like she did. Ray respected her business mentality and the fact that she never overstepped her boundaries. But right there, in that moment, the pain Ray saw on her face was almost unbearable. He pulled her into his wide chest and held her there. Adrianna clenched the back of Ray's suit jacket in her fists and buried her head in his long dreads. She could stay in his arms forever.

"Promise me that when you find out who did this," she whispered, "that you'll bleed them dry."

Ray's face was atop of her soft hair, but his eyes were on the graves. His little brother' deaths wouldn't be for nothing, he knew that.

"I promise."

The two separated, and with one last farewell to their brothers, they made their way to the waiting limousine.

"You OK, ma?" Devynn asked Adrianna when she sat down next to her.

"No," Adrianna answered truthfully as the limo pulled off, making its way to Ray's estate. "And I won't be until whoever did this is in a fuckin' body bag."

Everyone but Mocha nodded in agreement. Instead, she turned her head to look out the window.

"Where's Tyler?" Sadie asked her cousin, hoping he knew.

She'd called him a few times since they parted ways after touching down back in Detroit but received no answer or callback. Before Jamaica, she and Tyler didn't really talk like that, but she knew he wouldn't just automatically switch back into that mind state. Not after everything. She knew he was going to get Marie, but no one had heard from her either. She was surprised Ray wasn't livid when he didn't show up for D and Amann's funeral, but he said his man just didn't do funerals. That would be understandable, had it not been for the fact that Sadie saw the look on his face when Devynn delivered the news. Something was wrong; she could feel it in her gut. Ray's phone rang before he could give her an answer.

"Hello . . . This is him." Everyone in the back of the limo watched Ray's face drop even more than it had already been. There was a long pause as he listened. "He's alive? OK. Thank you."

Sadie was too afraid to ask him what was just said over the phone once the call was disconnected.

"What happened, Ray?" Devynn asked forcefully.

"They found Tyler's body this morning." Ray's lips moved, but every other feature was frozen in place. "Six bullet holes; one to the head. They got him in an induced coma."

He sucked his lips in and nodded his head. His best friend and his right-hand man. Whoever was behind the hits on The Last Kings had hit the wrong man. Sadie let out a small cry, and tears filled her eyes.

"One by one, they're killing us off," Devynn spoke in a low tone. "Who the fuck is doing this shit?"

No one spoke because no one had an answer. The only thought going through Sadie's mind was that she needed to get to the hospital Tyler was at. She needed to see him. The fact that he was still alive said nothing about how much longer he had to live. Any thoughts of Marie and her whereabouts fled her mind. All she cared about was him.

"Take me to the hospital," she called to Pierre.

"No," Ray said forcefully. He was taking charge. "Pierre, I want you to get Sadie, Mocha, and Devynn to my house. Adrianna, you come with me to the hospital."

"No!" Sadie screamed. "Fuck that shit! I have to see him, Ray. He needs me right now."

Adrianna looked into Sadie's tearstained, longing eyes and knew what she'd known since the beginning of The Last Kings. She loved Tyler, more than anything. After losing two of the loves of her life, she knew how unbearable the pain was, and the fact that she never got to say good-bye pushed the knife even further into her heart. Sadie had that chance if Tyler didn't make it, but she could tell that Ray's word was final.

"Sadie, shut the fuck up and listen to me." Ray raised his voice at Sadie, seeing her once again as his little cousin that he had to protect instead of his business partner. "That's three down! The safest place for all of you is my house. It's not negotiable."

Sadie knew she could argue and fight all she wanted, but Ray would make sure she got out of the car at the house, especially once she knew that Devynn would be given orders to not let her leave. Her heart was breaking all over again. She didn't want to lose Tyler right when she got him.

"Please," she whispered to her cousin. She knew he didn't understand, nor could she make him understand, but she *had* to go to that hospital.

Even though Ray knew Sadie cared about Tyler, his take on the matter at hand never altered. Niggas were going to war on him, and he had to make sure the ones he had left on his team were taken care of.

"No," he said finally. "I'll see you when I leave the hospital."

When they got to Ray's estate, he gave Sadie a hug and kissed her on the cheek. He did the same to Mocha, but she pulled away slightly. Ray and Adrianna switched to his Hummer and prepared to be en route to the hospital.

"Dev, make sure no one gets in . . . or out. And your guns . . . Make sure the safety is off 'em. I got niggas at the gate armed with orders to dead any unknown face. Be easy and I'm going to get at y'all in a minute."

Devynn nodded at her orders in the rounded driveway in front of Ray's huge brick estate. She looked back and saw Maria opening the door for Mocha and Sadie and turned back to him.

"You should let her go, Ray," she told him. "She loves him."

Ray nodded. "I know," he admitted.

He knew about everything. Ever since Sadie hit age eighteen, he noticed her budding infatuation with his right-hand man. He also noticed how Tyler's eyes lit up whenever Sadie entered the room. He had long since given them his blessing, but he knew that it would be up to them if they wanted to pursue it any further. Tyler was the only man that would be able to handle Sadie and take care of her the way only a boss could. He was the only man Ray trusted with her heart. That knowledge was the main reason why he would not allow Sadie to go see Tyler in the state he was in.

"I'll see y'all after I see what's up with my mans," Ray said and shook Devynn's hand like he would a nigga because that's how she preferred to be treated.

Devynn said one last good-bye to Adrianna and watched them drive away until they were completely out of sight.

Chapter 24

After Maria made dinner and we all had eaten, everyone ventured off into separate parts of the house. Devynn tried to make small talk with me, but Tyler was the only thing on my mind. I texted Ray and told him to call me as soon as he got there with Tyler's stats and the doctors' diagnosis. I lay posted in my window seat overlooking the view before I tired of that. I needed to take a long, hot bath to ease my mind. Dropping my pistol on my dresser, I headed for my bathroom. While running my bathwater, I heard the door to my room open and shut.

"You OK, Say?" I heard the familiar voice of Mocha ask.

I turned and looked at her and shook my head.

"Shit wasn't supposed to be like this, Mo," I said, still not able to believe D and Amann were gone, even though I'd seen them both in their caskets. "Kings don't die."

Mocha said nothing. She just came in and sat on the toilet.

"Niggas just popping up out of nowhere killing muhfuckas. We have never had bad business with anyone since the beginning, Mo, you know this. Pussy niggas can't even show who they are. I swear on my soul, for every bullet in Tyler's body, I'ma put in that nigga's dick. On God," I was going on a rant; I had to let it all out. "Kings. Don't. Fucking. Die. D and Amann were Kings, nigga, and that means they'll live on through me, you— shit, all of us. Fuck the bullshit; this shit ends tonight."

I finally took a breath and saw Mocha sitting with her eyes closed. Her long hair fell in front of her face, and her shoulders were hunched. She was shaking like she was crying, but I saw no tears. I went over to her and held her, knowing that she needed me.

"It's OK, Mo, we're going to get these niggas," I said into her hair.

She nodded her head and pushed me off of her. She then stood up and began to walk out of the bathroom door. Her back to me, she stopped midstride.

"I'm so sorry, Say," she said, and before I could ask her why, she ran out of the room.

I stared at the bathroom door for a second before I closed it. No one was in their right state of mind at that point. But I knew one thing for sure . . . We needed to get in it. We were all we had left, and an army needed their generals to be strong. I refused to lose my fuckin' city. I checked my phone to see if I had any message from Ray but saw nothing, so I knelt down to test the temperature of the water with my hand. Under me, I heard a loud thud, but I figured it was just Maria bustling around. I knew no one could ever make it past Ray's security. Then the door behind me opened, and I heard Mocha reenter the bathroom.

"What did Maria drop, Mo?" I asked her, and no sooner were the words out of my mouth did I hear gunfire from downstairs.

I jumped up to reach for my pistol. I knew that whoever it was, was there to try to finish the job that they started.

"Mocha—" I started as I swiveled around to tell her to follow me—but the person standing behind me wasn't Mocha. My heart dropped as I recognized the man behind me, and I dropped my gun.

"Not quite," the tall man said and smiled the evil smile I remembered like it was yesterday.

"N-no," I barely whispered. "You're dead!"

"Once again, not quite," the man said, and before I could do or say anything else, the butt of his gun came crashing into my temple, causing me to fall and hit my head on the edge of the tub.

I heard laughter and felt pain soar through my body just before everything went black.

Chapter 25

Ray and Adrianna rushed through the hospital doors to get to the room Tyler was in. At first, Ray was relieved to know that he was still alive, but once he saw him in his hospital bed, grief overwhelmed him. He went and sat in the chair beside him and listened to the light beeps of the machine he was strapped into. Adrianna stood back, allowing Ray time with his best friend. The top of Tyler's head was bandaged and so was the majority of his body. She knew only a true soldier could take six bullets and live to tell the tale—hopefully.

Ray clenched his fists while he looked over Tyler. His eyes were shut, and he was resting peacefully. When he asked the doctor what was the extent of Tyler's head injury, he received some good news. The bullet never penetrated his brain, and they were able to remove it from where it was embedded in his skull. The bad news was that Ray didn't know how he was going to tell him that Marie was missing.

"I always said you were hardheaded, fam." Ray shook his head at how fortunate Tyler was. He knew it was pure luck. No man would shoot another man that many times if he wasn't shooting to kill. "Don't trip though, bro, I got niggas out looking for the muhfuckas who did this to you, D, and Amann. Nobody is going to eat until I got the muhfuckas' hearts in my hands!"

Adrianna listened to the words and felt the power in them. She was in tune with every word and went to Ray and clasped his hand in hers. Tyler must have felt them too because his eyebrows furrowed, and he let out a low groan as he came out of his coma. His eyes opened a slit as he tried to focus on them, but couldn't, and they shut once more. Ray thought he was out again, but then Tyler's mouth moved like he was speaking, but no words came out.

"Tyler," Adrianna said softly at his futile attempt to speak. "You need to rest. You have some pretty serious injuries."

Tyler ignored her and still tried to talk.

"Alanna," he kept repeating in a gurgled voice. "For Alanna."

"Alanna?" Adrianna whispered to Ray. "Who's Alanna?"

Ray shrugged and tried to listen more intently to what his mans was saying.

"Fram Atlanna," Tyler tried again eyes, clenched shut.

"Fram Atlanna?" Ray repeated. "From Atlanta! Ty, nigga, what you saying, man?"

Ray hoped Tyler would be able to muster more, and he leaned forward to ensure that he missed nothing. Tyler took a lot of deep breaths in between his words, but what he had to say was important, even though he was pushing himself and using all of his nonexistent energy.

"Took Marie. From Atlanta . . . business. Khiron," Tyler was able to get out before his monitor started going crazy, and he started coughing up blood.

An array of doctors and nurses rushed in to tend to him. Ray and Adrianna were ushered from the room, but Ray had heard all that he needed to hear. Khiron was behind all of it. He should have known, remembering Khiron's last words to him. Ray knew he must have been holding Marie hostage or something. Her body should have turned up already if she was dead. But why? Marie had never been a part of their operation,

Tyler made sure of that. But what Ray knew was that if she was indeed still alive, her life was on a countdown, and Ray had to find her before her time was up. One thing Ray should have kept in mind after the meeting with Khiron was *never underestimate your opponents.*

Never.

Now that he knew it was Khiron, he thought back to the meeting at Amore. He kept seeing Khiron's eyes shift downward. He thought that he was just observing his surroundings, but when he thought more in-depth about it, from Khiron's seat, he had the perfect view of the entrance to the underground club. Also, as soon as Khiron left, D and Amann made the drop-off. If he was the one who set up the hit at Lace, then that meant his people saw D and Amann remove the money being harbored there, and *that* meant he watched them take it to Amore. Ray was sure Khiron was already mad about the whole denial of business thing, which made Amann and D the perfect targets, their affiliation to The Last Kings branded proudly on their arms. Ray almost choked on his air while his thoughts spiraled inside of his head. How could he have been so naïve? The nigga was coming at their necks. He wanted the city, but he could only have it over Ray's dead body . . . and Ray didn't plan on dying.

"I need to get to Amore," Ray said, turning to walk down the long hallway in the hospital. "This nigga is dead. Stay here with Tyler and keep me posted."

"Khiron . . . Khiron . . . Khiron!" Adrianna repeated to herself until she remembered where she'd heard that name from.

Before he went to Jamaica, she remembered Tyler talking to somebody with that name from Atlanta and setting up a meeting with Ray. Ray didn't put him on, so that was a reason to be bitter—but to start a war? There had to be more to it.

"Ray, wait!" she yelled and ran after him. "Don't do anything stupid. Please."

Ray turned on his heels and looked down at her. "This nigga is going to pay, ma," Ray told her, rage in his eyes. "Two of my bros are dead, and this nigga is somewhere prancing around my muhfuckin' city making his claim! I'ma show this nigga kings don't fuckin' die. Say it!"

"Kings don't die," she said up at him. "We live on forever. I'm coming with you, Ray. You need me."

"Nah, ma." Ray grabbed her hands. "Hold it down here for me, a'ight?"

Before Adrianna could protest, Ray's lips were on hers. Their tongues tasted each other for the first time, and neither one wanted to let go. Their embrace was one so precious that when Ray finally let her go, Adrianna had tears in her eyes.

"Promise me I'll see you again," she said.

Ray chuckled. "I promise," he smiled down at her. "And when I come back, you're going to have to pack your bags because we're going away for a while."

In light of everything going on, Adrianna somehow reached inside and pulled a smile out.

"Here," she reached under her skirt and handed Ray her chrome 9-mm pistol. "I want one of my bullets in that muhfucka."

Ray nodded his head and instead of saying good-bye, he planted a kiss on her forehead and left her standing alone in the hallway. Adrianna then turned back to the hospital room that Tyler was in. She stayed outside of the room and looked in through the window, watching the nurses get Tyler situated once more. His eyes opened for a brief second and locked on hers before they put him under again. Her eyes fell on her Last Kings tattoo on her foot, and she nodded her head.

"Hang in there, Ty," she whispered. "Kings don't die."

Inside of her Chanel clutch, she felt her cell phone vibrating. Seeing it was Devynn, she answered it immediately.

"Hello?" she answered.

"So-somebody set us up!" Devynn choked into the phone.

"What? Where are you?" Adrianna's heart froze over, and she listened to Devynn cough into the phone.

"I got away, but Mocha and Sadie were taken, yo," Devynn struggled to get out. "Ray's guards turned A. Them niggas set us up! They let the niggas *walk right in*."

Adrianna went into a Spanish rant, cursing everyone walking the earth at that moment.

"Bitch, English! They blasted Maria as soon as she opened the door, and I was next," Devynn informed her. "If I ain't have on my vest, I'd be dead too. Where's Ray? Let that nigga know his team ain't loyal no more."

Ray . . . Adrianna forgot all about him. She took off in the direction he'd gone, phone still on her ear listening to Devynn.

"It was Khiron!" Adrianna told Devynn while looking frantically around the hospital for Ray. She hopped on the elevator to hopefully catch him in the parking lot.

"That nigga from Atlanta?" Devynn asked. "Fuck! I told Tyler not to welcome that bitch into the city!"

Adrianna finally reached the hospital parking lot but had no luck in finding Ray.

"Shit!" she yelled out. "Where you at, Dev?"

"I took one of Ray's cars. I'm on my way to the hospital. Almost there now."

"I'm in the parking lot. Hurry up. We have to get to Amore!"

Chapter 26

The sound of static aroused me. My eyes opened, but everything around me was a blur. I could slightly see a TV on, but nothing was on the screen but a piece of paper. I didn't move until my vision came in all the way, and when it did, I noticed all familiar surroundings. I was lying down on a soft twin bed in a tank top and a pair of shorts. There was no light on in the room but a little ray beamed through a window above my head. Looking around, I saw all of my stuffed animals atop a chestnut dresser. It was a sight I saw every day in the morning when I woke up at . . . Grandma Rae's house! I jumped out of the bed but was floored almost the same exact second. The pain I felt in my head was unbearable, but I still crawled to the bedroom door. There was light seeping into the room from under the door, but I saw no shadows or heard no form of life. I struggled to my feet and tried to snatch the door open. No luck. It was locked from the other side.

"What's happening?" I said aloud to myself backing away from the door. "Grandma Rae? Grandma Rae!" I called.

As I backed away from the door, my foot got caught on something, and I fell backward with a loud thud. My hands felt around for the cause of my fall, and I shuddered when they found what they were looking for. I did something I didn't know I was capable of doing. I screamed. I screamed a bloodcurdling scream because my hands recognized the cold, clammy face they were placed on. Eyes, lips, and nose . . . When my hands reached the familiar texture of hair and felt that the back of the head was completely gone—I lost it.

"No! No! No!" I cried and clutched my grandmother's stiff body. "I'm so sorry, Grandma Rae. I love you. I'm so sorry!"

I didn't care that her body was cold and lifeless or that I was lying in a pool of blood. I lay there for what seemed like forever crying. When I finally did look up, my eyes, blurry once again from crying, fell on the television. I didn't notice until then that there was a note stuck to it. Arms shaking, I let my grandma's body go and stood to my feet. I flipped on the light switch in the room, but instantly wished I hadn't. Blood was splattered all over the wall in my old room, letting me know it was where my grandmother's murder was committed. I looked down at my clothes and saw blood there too. I'd seen many dead bodies in the past year; I even helped add to them, but seeing my grandmother's body brought on a strong urge to vomit. My heart broke inside of my chest, and I couldn't do anything but turn my head toward the television. I took a deep breath and stepped over Grandma Rae's body. I crept to the television, keeping an eye on the door, half-expecting whoever was keeping me there to burst through and kill me next. No one did. I snatched the note off of the TV screen, unfolded it, and looked blankly at the tiny words staring back at me.

Press Play.

I glanced up at the VCR that sat atop the television and saw that a little green light was shining, indicating that it was powered on. Trembling at what I was about to witness, my finger found its way to the play button and applied a tiny amount of pressure. The screen changed from static to footage of a bedroom. The camera appeared to be perched on someone's bedroom dresser pointing at a king-sized bed. The lights in the room were dimmed, but there was something vaguely familiar about the room. My stomach was slowly dropping as I tried to make sense of what I was seeing on the screen. The room was clearly a large one, but I could only see what the camera showed me. I couldn't see the door to the room, but I heard it open and shut. What I heard next was enough to twist my falling stomach into knots.

"Please stop! I don't want it," a young girl's voice pleaded.

She began backing up unknowingly into the view of the camera wearing only a nightgown. She was brown skinned. Her hair, long and straight, hung disheveled from her head. She was average height, and although she had the curves of a grown woman, she couldn't have been more than fourteen. She turned facing the camera as a man entered the view as well. The sharpness in her eyes was clouded by the tears dripping down the high cheekbones on her pretty face. I gasped as I stared at myself in disbelief—floored at the sickening realization that Nino had filmed the things he did to me . . . and I never knew.

It was like reliving a nightmare . . . I didn't feel like I was watching it; I felt like I was there all over again . . .

"Nino, please don't!" I begged my mother's man in a meek voice. "I do everything you ask me to. Just don't hurt me anymore."

I backed up until I stumbled backward on my king-sized bed. I knew pleading with him would do nothing just by seeing the hungry look in his eyes. He would still take my womanhood, something I never gave willingly— just like he did every other night.

"Naw . . ." Nino licked his lips while parting my thighs. "That pussy is too tight to pass up."

"But you promised, Nino! You promised! You said if I put in more work than your best trapper you would stop!"

I was sobbing by then just at the mere thought of the broken promise. The promise was what drove me to hustle harder than any nigga Nino had patrolling the streets. In one month, I single-handedly racked in a little over twenty racks. I should have known the man who had the gumption enough to stick his dick inside his lady's fourteen-year-old daughter wouldn't keep his word. Nino began laughing, showing his pearly whites. Women went crazy over Nino, but his gorgeous outer layer was outshined by the evil content of his heart.

"Mom," I whispered as he loomed over me unstrapping his belt and dropping his pants.

"Your mom is somewhere in this fuckin' house passed out, li'l shorty. She ain't worried about you." He dropped to his knees, grinning at the sight of my fat lips under my nightgown. "Damn, I guess it's true what they say. Like mother, like daughter."

Nino roughly finished parting my legs as I lay there just staring at the ceiling, wishing I was anywhere but there. I braced myself for the feeling of disgust soon to come. My tears were warm as they rolled freely down my temples into my hair. I closed my eyes and tried to enter a world where no one could hurt me. Nino tore my panties off and lifted my gown just enough so my bottom half was completely visible to the world.

"I'm about to give you your first squirting orgasm," he whispered and began slowly massaging my engorged clitoris with his thumb.

Don't get wet, don't get wet, I thought, but my body didn't pay me any mind. My vagina had a mind of its own, and I could feel my juices start flowing.

I hated Nino. I hated my hate for Nino. Over the period of time that he'd been raping me, he took an even more twisted take on the matter. He didn't want me to fight it; instead, he made it his job to find each and every way to give me pleasure. He'd made me come more times than I could count, and I despised myself for it. With every blissful feeling and every drop of juice dripping from in between my thighs, I died a little bit more inside.

"Yea," Nino whispered to me, still working his thumb. "You know you like this shit, girl. Go 'head and make that pussy soak for Daddy's dick."

Nino watched in amazement at how wet I was becoming, and I clenched my eyes shut, refusing to enjoy the malicious act being committed against my womanhood. Where was my mother? She knew what Nino did to me. She should be there stopping him! Instead, she got high, so she couldn't hear my screams for help. She'd thrown me under the bus for the man that supported her habit, and even so, I couldn't help but to love her.

Nino's tongue caught me by surprise, and my body jerked. His tongue was beating my clit like a drum, and it took every ounce of self-control I had left not to moan. Instead, I sobbed louder. I cried as he devoured my tender spot because it felt so good, and I knew it was so wrong. His hands gripped my thighs tightly while he flicked his hot tongue in and out of me. When he was done, he smacked his lips like he'd just finished a full-course meal and stood up. His erection pointed straight out, making his boxers look like a tent. He smiled sinisterly down at me, and I cringed, knowing what was about to happen next. He dropped his boxers and began stroking his beast. His dick was big—nine inches long and at least three inches wide—and I often wondered why he wanted me. He could have any woman he desired, but yet, he was in my bedroom every night.

"You ready, baby?" he spoke to me like his lover, not a child.

He lifted my nightgown over my head, exposing my already full breasts. His hands palmed each one, and his fingers skillfully massaged the tips of my engorged nipples.

"I hate you," I whispered.

My tears stopped flowing as I accepted my fate, just like every other time. His hands were soft on my skin, but I flinched with every touch. The tips of his fingers trailed down my body until they rested on my hips, gripping them as he prepared to enter me raw. Nino put me on birth control when he first started fucking me to ensure that I didn't get pregnant. He hated condoms, and he also had a fetish for nutting in my "young pussy." Leaving his mark.

"You hate me?" he asked and slid all nine inches inside of me without a warning.

The thrust was powerful and awakened every sensation my walls had, causing them to clench tightly around his shaft. My back arched, and I clenched my eyes shut at the pain. He thrust again . . . and again. Until the pain subsided only to be replaced by a pleasure so strong I had to bit my lip. Nino placed his mouth by my ear and began whispering things. He told me how beautiful I was and how good it felt inside of me.

"You're so beautiful, shorty," he said over and over as he hit it harder with every stroke. "This shit is dripping, ma!"

I tried to keep my hands limp at my sides while he defiled my body, but soon, they were gripping his shoulders as he rode me to ecstasy.

Sadie, no, I thought. Don't like it. Don't like—

"Ahh!" *I moaned loudly into his ear when he used his fingers to roughly pinch my right nipple.*

He was diving in so deep, every thrust thumped my love box; soon it was going to burst.

"This is my pussy," he panted into my ear. "You hear me, girl? You belong to me! Fuuck! This shit is tight."

When it came to Nino, it was a hit and miss. Some nights he was rough and abusive. Other nights, he was sweet and sensual, like a boyfriend. But he wasn't. He was a rapist. I despised the fact that I was enjoying it. My hips began throwing it at him, matching him stroke for stroke.

"Yea, I knew you liked this shit, girl! Throw it up at Daddy!"

My pussy liked it; I didn't. My mind was screaming to stop; but my body was saying keep going. When I felt my orgasm coming, I tried my hardest to stop it, but that made it come even harder. I screamed, and my eyes rolled to the back of my head. It felt like I was peeing, but I knew I wasn't. Nino pumped three more times before pulling his penis out with his hand and squirting his nut all over my face and hair.

"You ain't shit, bitch," he said coldly standing over me. "You ain't never going to be shit either. If I tell you to get out there and trap, that's what the fuck you're going to do. If I want some pussy, you're going to part them legs for Daddy. I own you, bitch. You and your momma, and if you don't do what I say, I will blow ya' fucking heads off."

I turned my head from the scene being played on the television. I couldn't bear to watch any more. I couldn't watch the younger tortured me tremble any longer. Whoever had taken me knew about my past . . . Nino? It couldn't have been. I saw him die. My heart was beating hard, and I was panicking. Although fear was present in my heart, anger was too. Without thinking, I pushed the TV off of the desk that it was placed on. There was a loud crash and glass covered the floor. I snatched the VCR up and flung it against the wall, shattering it into a dozen pieces.

"Fuck you!" I screamed to my captors, fists balled.

I was becoming hysterical. I didn't know how long I'd been passed out, and I wasn't going to be contained like a fucking animal for some sick pervert's entertainment. I wondered if Ray knew I was missing. What if he didn't? I wasn't strapped. I was defenseless. Under the door I saw a shadow moving and heard footsteps. I looked around my room for anything to defend myself and came up short. Keys jingled, and I heard the lock on the door click, allowing whoever was on the other side entrance. The door slowly opened until the gape was wide enough to step through. The person who stepped through was very handsome, dressed in regular street clothes, and the resemblance between him and the demon from my past was uncanny. I couldn't help it. I took a few steps back away from him. My knees buckled, and I felt like the helpless fourteen-year-old girl I once was.

"N-Nino?" I asked, not believing my eyes.

His curls sat atop of my captor's head perfectly, just like Nino's. The skin complexion all the way down to the way he stood was Nino. The man smiled at me and shook his head.

"Nah, ma." He stepped closer, and I focused my eyes, realizing that it wasn't the man from my nightmares after all. The man began walking toward me, stepping over Grandma Rae's dead body. "My name is Khiron, not that it matters."

"Khiron?" I asked confused.

That was the name of the man Tyler set up to meet with Ray. But why?

"I've been waiting for this moment for a *long* time, Sadie," he said softly as he advanced on me. I saw the butt of his pistol poking through his muscle shirt so I knew rushing him would be the move of a dumb bitch.

"When Ray finds out—" I started, but was cut off by loud laughter.

"Not even Ray can save you now, bitch. I've been waiting for this shit for six fuckin' years!"

Khiron looked down at the broken television and the glass from the screen that was scattered on the blood-stained carpet. He stopped an arm's length in front of me with his head cocked.

"What . . . You didn't like my little home movie? Or should I say, *your* little home movie?" he chuckled. "Damn, shorty, you was a freak, though. I can see why Nino kept biting."

The knots in my stomach tightened. My past, something that I thought was over, had finally caught up to me. I knew he was the one behind all of the havoc being caused in the city, but none of it added up. Ray denied business with him, so the fuck what? That couldn't have been it.

"Why are you doing this?" I cut my eyes at him. "Ray is going to kill you."

"Ray doesn't even know what the fuck is going on, bitch. How can you call yourself a kingpin and don't even know what the fuck is going on in your own city? He ain't shit but a fuck nigga, but he's just icing on the cake. You, Sadie? You're the big fish I've been wanting. It was one hell of a coincidence too! When that bitch-ass nigga told me I couldn't hold his product, I was going to just chill. But then I found out he worked with the Italians. I couldn't just leave. Not without taking what's rightfully mine."

"What the fuck are you talking about?" I yelled into his face. "And how did you get those tapes?"

The house burned down. I saw it. There was no way anything could have been preserved . . . least of all, Nino's sick, fetish tapes. Who the fuck was this nigga, and how did he know about my past? Khiron's cold stare turned distant and foggy.

"You were all he ever talked about. He always told me how hustle lived in your heart . . . and how much of a waste it was on a little bitch like you." Khiron was talking and my mind was reaching, trying to grasp his words. "Imagine my frustration. Being in the shadow of someone I never even met! I was nineteen and on the verge of in-heriting an empire bigger than you could ever dream! But because of you, I was held back from it because somehow, you could put in more work than me. That made me . . ." Khiron paused and snapped his fingers. "Now, what was the word he used? Aw yea, that's right, *incompetent*."

Without warning, he struck me in my face so hard I felt my jaw crack. I fell to the ground with a loud thud, and he walked up and kicked me hard in my ribs. I felt blood flow from my mouth, and I spit it out, clutching my stomach where I lay. Khiron began pacing back and forth in front of me, and he continued with his story.

"Bitch! I remember the last time he came to visit me. It was the weekend. Summer vacation just started, and he was meeting with an Italian connect in Atlanta, but something was wrong with him. The nigga was jumpy, and a boss is never jumpy. When he left, it was in a hurry, and he forgot his duffle bag. I called it his duffle bag of secrets. He never even said good-bye."

He stopped pacing and knelt down in front of my aching face. I was confused. Why would Khiron care about a good-bye from another nigga? I struggled to sit up to face him, my mind reeling. I thought back to

Nino's monthly trips to Atlanta. I knew he went there because he ran big business there, but he also went there to visit . . . Something in my mind clicked, and my heart froze over.

"You're his son," I whispered, wide-eyed. "You're Nino's son."

I couldn't believe how naïve I'd been. The resemblance between Khiron and Nino was undeniable. Nino always called Khiron "Khy" when he spoke about him, so I never knew his full name . . . I did now, though. Khiron's distant look was replaced with coldness once again, and he grabbed me by my hair. He studied my face.

"Finding out my pops had a thing for young pussy was a little disturbing. That shit was sick, especially since he was still fuckin' my mom, but I still watched the tapes." He yanked my head so that his mouth was directly on my ear, and he spoke in a soft, taunting tone. "I watched you beg and scream and cry over and over. He had cameras in his office too, Sadie . . ."

His voice trailed off and echoed in my head.

No, I thought, shaking my head, knowing what he was saying.

My mind took me back to the day I'd broken into Nino's office. I was so clouded with anger that day six years ago that I'd been careless. I never would have thought Nino would be sick enough to record the malicious acts he did with me, but I should have known that his office was under surveillance. Khiron let go of my hair and leaned back to get a good look at the expression on my face.

"Priceless," he said. "Yea, bitch, I knew it was you who had my pops killed. Snitch! You killed everything, bitch!"

Khiron kicked me again and more blood came up. I knew that unless some sort of miracle happened, I was going to be murdered. I never in a million years thought that the son of the man I had killed would come out looking to spill blood. I felt tears rush to my eyes as the reality hit me. It was my fault D and Amann were dead. Khiron was toying with me. He was enjoying seeing me suffer.

"Where's Mocha?" I asked with a mouth full of salty blood. "And Devynn?"

"Devynn is dead. Bitch took a shotgun shell to the chest," Khiron laughed, and tears came to my eyes.

Devynn and I weren't the closest, but she was a real bitch and a true soldier. She didn't deserve to die.

"You bitch!" I screamed. "They didn't do anything to you! Why did you kill them?"

"All of you have to die," he shrugged. "I'm taking Detroit. Fuck a business deal."

"No!" I yelled. "Where's Mocha?"

I was afraid of what he was going to say. I would take his gun and dead myself if he told me she'd met the same fate as Devynn.

"Don't trip, shorty," Khiron said, his Georgia drawl strong. "That bitch is probably on a yacht chilling, eating crab cakes or some shit."

"Stop lyin', nigga! Where is she?" I snarled, rushing him, only to receive a blow harder than the first one.

"It's funny that you're worried about ya homegirl when *she's* the one who gave up your whereabouts. She's the one who brought me here to Grandma's house, who, I might add, was one feisty old bitch. You wanna know where she is?"

Khiron came to where my body was laid out next to Grandma Rae's and once again grabbed the back of my tussled hair, forcing my head up to look at him. All three of him. As my eyes tried to focus on his face, I heard somebody else enter the room.

"You wanna know where she is, Sadie?" Khiron yelled, pulling my hair so hard I felt some rip away from my scalp.

"Yes," I said weakly, cringing in pain.

"I'm right here," a voice so familiar to me said.

I didn't want to believe the owner of the voice was my ride-or-die bitch. My day one. But when my eyes averted to the figure standing in the doorway, I knew it was real. My vision was blurry, and my mind slightly out of it, but I could spot Mocha from a mile away. She was my best friend. *Was.* The betrayal I felt was so powerful, it hurt physically. The hurt I felt overpowered the anger. Mocha stood over where I was , bleeding in a mixture of my own and Grandma Rae's blood in a designer dress and open-toe stilettos. She looked like a celebrity. Khiron threw my head back down viciously, almost causing me to black out again before standing up. Through my clouded vision, I watched him walk to Mocha and kiss her sloppily on her mouth. She let him for a second, but then she pushed him off of her.

"This isn't how it was supposed to happen, Khiron!" I could hear in her voice that she was starting to cry. "You promised me you wouldn't hurt her!"

Khiron laughed.

"Baby, I'm a dope man. That was *your* mistake if you believed me. This is what I do. If you have a problem, you can join this bitch in the afterlife," he told her. When she was quiet, he continued. "This bitch killed my pops! *This* is the bitch responsible for taking *my* empire, baby! Aw, yea, I'm killing this bitch!"

I used all of my strength to sit up and stare into Mocha's eyes. A huge knot was forming on the right side of my face, but I ignored the screeching pain.

"Why, Mocha?" I asked. "Why would you turn on us?"

"I-I love him, Sadie," Mocha said what only a weak bitch would and shrugged her shoulders meekly. "He promised me a life outside of the drug ring. A life of riches without having to put in any work. You know that's all I ever wanted! This was *your* dream, Say! *Not mine!*"

"You could have had that, Mocha!" I screamed, letting the tears fall. "At any fucking time! I would have had you! You let this snake-ass nigga know where we laid our heads—for what? So you could go shopping all day and sit at home? You're going to let him take everything for your own selfishness. Fuck you, Mocha. When he kills me, don't even mourn my death because you're *already* dead to me."

Mocha's eyes went wide at my words and a sob escaped her mouth.

"All those trips to Atlanta." I shook my head at how dumb I'd been to trust her. That's how she met Khiron. She was his key to me.

I stared at Mocha disgusted that she'd chosen dick over me. She was like my sister. Blood couldn't have made us any closer. I trusted her with everything I had, and there she was, staring down at me in my demise. She looked at Grandma Rae and turned her head so she couldn't see her until she stepped over her to get to me. She dropped on her knees and grasped my hands.

"It wasn't supposed to be like this, Say." Her lips trembled when she spoke. "I'm sorry."

I pulled my hands from hers and spat in her face.

"Fuck you," I said and meant it.

Mocha stared into my eyes for a few more moments, and I saw her heart break. I knew she saw mine break too.

"No." She shook her head and stood up and ran up on Khiron, swinging her fists. "You're not going to kill her! We had a deal!"

"It's too late, Mocha!" Khiron grabbed her and threw her hard to the side. He pulled his .45 from his waist and advanced on me again. "You're going to live and watch what you caused. You won't get the luxury of death, bitch."

He aimed the chrome barrel at me and fired once, catching me in my leg. I'd never been shot before, and the pain was excruciating, but I didn't scream. I fell back and tried to stomach the pain.

"No, Khiron!" I heard Mocha scream, and a bullet hole appeared inches away from my head.

"Get off me!" Khiron said, and I heard another thud and a grunt from Mocha.

I turned my head in time to see Khiron coming for me, and I tried to get up, but the pressure from Khiron's foot on my chest prevented that from being possible. So I laughed. I laughed like a crazed person, and I saw the look of confusion on his face. I was about to die. I knew it, but my mouth still worked perfectly fine.

"You think you can kill me, bitch?" I said through clenched teeth. "Kings. Don't. Fucking. Die!! You will *never* be near as much of a boss as me. Even your punk-ass daddy knew that! Fuck that nigga too. I'm glad I had him killed, and guess what? No matter what happens here . . . you'll be next!"

The pressure of Khiron's foot lessened, and he stared down at me as I laughed. His lip upturned, and he aimed his gun at my heart.

"You took everything from me, so I'm going to do the same thing to you. You're going to burn. And Ray? I'm about to kill him too."

I saw Khiron's jaw clench just before he pulled the trigger twice more, and I felt heat in my chest and in my stomach.

"R-Ray," was all I could get out before I began choking on my own blood.

"N-n-nooooo!!!" Mocha screamed and tried to get to me.

Khiron strong-armed her and held her back. He grinned at me, enjoying the sight of me dying slowly. The world around me was becoming dim, and I knew my life that remained on the earth was short. I coughed on the blood that spilled from my mouth, and the pain in my chest was unbearable. My hands clutched my stomach, trying to catch the blood, but there was so much of it, it was no use. I just wanted the pain to stop.

"Sadie, I'm so sorry!" Mocha screamed. "Why? No! No! No!"

Her voice grew distant, and my eyes closed. The pain was slowly subsiding, and my last thought before everything went black was Grandma Rae's voice.

"Sadie, you're my special baby. You have a special heart, you hear? You're going to do great things in this world. My special girl, you make this world. Don't you let it make you."

I let go of the little piece of life I was holding on to in sorrow with sadness and comfort that soon Ray would be joining me.

Chapter 27

Ray entered Amore and immediately knew something was up. It was empty. Top and bottom levels. No one was there, not even his workers. It was so quiet he would have been able to hear a pin drop. Gun raised, he went to the secret entrance of the club that was in the basement and found where all of his workers were. They were all sprawled out on the floor—dead, his money and product on the ground around them.

"Ray," he heard a voice whisper behind him, and as soon as he turned around to click on the owner, something hit him in the head so hard that he fell to the ground, blacked out.

When Ray finally opened his eyes, it felt as if no time had passed, but his body felt different. He looked around and the dead bodies of his employees let him know he was still in the same place. But when he tried to move his body, he found he couldn't. Looking down, he saw that he was bound tightly to a chair, and no matter how hard he tried to fight against the ropes, he couldn't get free. Around him he saw that he was encircled by a group of men. He recognized none of their faces, nor did he see a Last Kings tattoo anywhere on their bodies.

"There's no point, fam," Ray heard a vaguely familiar voice say. "You ain't gettin' free."

Ray's head whipped around, looking for the source of the voice, but with his head injury, that just made him dizzy.

"Who the fuck is there?" he called out angry that he'd been caught slipping.

"I told you I'd be seeing you, Ray," the voice said. "You know who the fuck it is."

Ray heard footsteps behind him, then a man appeared in front of him. Khiron stood over him like a man gloating over a big trophy fish that he'd just caught. And that's exactly what Ray was.

"I'm not going to make this last too long. I've already gotten what I wanted," Khiron smiled evilly at Ray. "This shit was too easy; easier than I expected. Glad you waited until I got here to come around to your senses. This should be fun now."

He laughed out loud and looked above Ray for a split second.

"You have a really nice house, by the way," he taunted. "I burned it down, of course."

Ray fought harder against the rope around his wrists and ankles but only tired himself. Sadie was in that house. If he'd burned it down with her in it . . .

"Don't worry," Khiron chuckled, pulling up a chair in front of Ray and taking a seat. "She was alive when we left the house."

The sick smile he wore like a shirt gave Ray a queasy feeling.

"Where are they?" Ray growled in a low voice. His tone was deadly. "Where are Mocha, Devynn, and Sadie?"

"Devynn is dead. I had no use for that bitch." Khiron shrugged his smile still planted on his face. "And Mocha? Well, see for yourself. Mocha!"

Mocha then too appeared in front of Ray, confusing him, and when he saw the tears in her eyes, he knew something was wrong.

"I'm so sorry, Ray," she whispered.

"Tell him where Sadie is, Mocha." Khiron grabbed her and pulled her so that she was sitting on his lap looking directly at Ray. "Tell him about how you gave me the directions to his home. Tell him about how you brought me to his grandmother's house, and how I blew the back of her head off. Tell him about how you watched me put the bullet in Sadie's heart."

Mocha was shaking as she stared into Ray's eyes and watched him fight against his restraints at the news he'd just received. That was the only time that she'd ever seen him look any form of weak. He'd always been their rock, their savior. He stopped fighting after a while and looked tired and beat. His dreads hung loosely around his slumped shoulders, and his eyes instantly were filled with pain at Khiron's words. He knew they were true by the tears rolling down Mocha's face and the sobs she was choking on. Ray was about to speak, but he had no words to say. He looked around at his establishment and the thousands of dollars on the ground and shook his head. His eyes fell on the entrance of the club, and he saw Devynn and Adrianna's faces. Devynn had her guns out, ready to rain fire on them all, but he shook his head slightly. If they entered the room, they would surely be dead, especially since Khiron already thought Devynn was. He saw tears form in Adrianna's eyes, and he thought of his promise to her. Promises, in his eyes, were never meant to be broken, especially if they were made by him. But at that moment, he knew that was the only promise he made in his life that he wouldn't be able to keep.

"You shot her in her heart?" Ray turned his attention back to Khiron. "In my grandmother's house?"

He was trying to send Devynn and Adrianna a subliminal message. *Get to that house.* Saving him was a lost cause unless they all wanted to die together. His eyes averted back to Mocha, and he spat on her in disgust.

"I took you in because of your loyalty to my cousin. You both better hope that whatever bullet enters my body kills me, or may God have mercy on ya' fucking souls . . . because I won't. And I *know* she won't."

Khiron laughed at the man before him, ignoring his comment.

"I thought about shooting you, but that's so old-fashioned, don't you think, my nigga?" Khiron pushed Mocha off of his lap, and one of the men surrounding them grabbed her by her arm to restrain her just in case she got out of control. "I want to watch you scream. I brought down the best! The Italians are going to have to find another flunky bitch. Look up."

Ray did as he was told and looked at what Khiron had glanced at earlier. Hanging from the ceiling was a huge bucket, and a rope was attached to it. Ray's eyes followed the rope and saw that one of Khiron's goons was holding the other end of it, an evil glint in his eyes.

"Acid." Khiron stood up and backed away. "There won't even be a skeleton when we're finished here."

"No! Please, Khiron, don't!" Mocha begged trying to fight against the man holding her.

Ray's eyes locked on Adrianna's, and he smiled. They would never know what could have been . . . what *should* have been. Adrianna covered her mouth when Khiron gave the man the signal to let go of the rope and turned her head into Devynn's shoulder just before the liquid hit Ray's body. There was a spine-tingling scream, but it belonged to Mocha, not Ray. He wasn't going to give Khiron the satisfaction. He felt his body burning and the pain was unbearable. It didn't take long for the acid to start to eat away at his flesh, and when Adrianna looked again, she saw his head slump. Ray was no more. It felt like her heart had been ripped out of her chest and thrown into the acid that killed him.

"And that, ladies and gentlemen," Khiron whispered just loud enough to be heard, "is how you take over an empire."

Epilogue

"Sadie?" I stared at the woman I'd believed was dead for a year in disbelief.

The eyes of my former best friend had changed. There was emptiness there. Although my gun was in my hand, I was too petrified to pull it on her. I felt like I was looking into the eyes of a ghost.

"H-How?" I saw her die. I *saw* Khiron kill her!

"What?" Sadie said her voice soft and cold as she cocked her head slightly at me. "You want a fuckin' hug? What's the matter, Mo? You look like you just saw a ghost!"

There was something different in her demeanor. The golden pharaoh on her forearm glistened in the night, indicating who her allegiance was still to and would forever be with.

"Sadie, I'm so sorry." I spoke the same words to her flesh right then and there that I thought her spirit was hearing every night. "I never wanted any of that to happen. It wasn't supposed to be like that."

I felt tears welling up in my eyes as I stared into the blankness in hers. The expression on her face let me know that she could care less about my words. They meant nothing to her. I noticed the black gloves on her hands and instantly knew why she was there. I let my grip loosen on Lucy. The remorse I felt for the fall of The Last Kings was unbearable. It was six cartels in one, and because of me, it was over. Instead, the only work that was seen in Detroit was the weak shit Khiron had going. Sadie's gaze wavered, and for a split second, I saw the rage that was held inside.

"You want to know how I survived, huh?" Sadie chuckled. "You should have paid more attention to Grandma Rae. I have a special heart, Mocha . . . You remember her saying that?"

I nodded my head. She said it every day, but I didn't see how it was relevant.

"The bullet Khiron put in my chest didn't penetrate it. My heart is on the *opposite* side of my chest, unlike the common person. That's what she meant by saying my heart was special. I found that out after being shot. If Khiron was smart, he would have put more than three bullets in my body; his mistake. But then again, if it hadn't been for Adrianna and Devynn showing up when they did, I would have been dead—no question. It took six months of physical therapy and being connected to fuckin' tubes to fully function again."

Distantly, I remembered Ray's last words:

"May God have mercy on ya' fucking souls . . . because I won't. And I know she won't."

"Did it make you happy?" Sadie asked me calmly. "Watching Ray die?"

All I could do was let the tears roll down my face and shake my head.

"We took you in, Mocha!" Sadie's eyes ripped me into shreds. "Bitch, you didn't have one person to live for, and we gave you that! But then, you choose a nigga over us? Over *family*? I don't have anybody now, Mocha. Not Grandma Rae, not Ray. Nobody!" Sadie began walking toward me, a fire burning in her eyes. "My cousin couldn't even receive a proper burial because there was *nothing* left to bury. And for what? For *this*?"

Sadie waved her arms around the neighborhood as her heels stabbed the ground with each step she took.

"Bitch, this nigga got you living out of a fuckin' shoe box ho'ing on the low." Sadie shook her head in pity. "I could dead your ass, and trust me, it's *so* tempting, but I'm not going to."

My mouth opened, not understanding. If I was her, I wouldn't even be having a conversation with me at all. I would have just put a bullet in my brain.

"I can't kill you, actually," Sadie smirked at me. "Just like Khiron used you as his key, *I'm* using you as mine. And I need you to lead me to someone."

"Y-your key to what? And lead you to who?" I found my voice again.

"Kings don't fucking die, remember, Mocha?" Sadie was directly in front of my face. "And there's a peasant running my fucking city. I need it back. Marie's missing. I know she's not dead. Tyler isn't going to rest until he finds her."

She nodded down the street, and I noticed an all-black Hummer. Ray's bulletproof Hummer posted.

"Tyler's alive?" I breathed, not believing it. I'd seen his obituary in the newspaper.

"You're not stupid, Mocha. You know what's up. We had to keep a low profile. But now, it's time to take back what's ours, and *you're* going to help." Sadie turned her back on me and began to walk away, but then stopped and turned her head slightly. "This meeting? It never happened. The *real* war starts tomorrow. Play your role. You'll be hearing from me soon. Oh, and don't worry, if this doesn't work, I *will* kill you, then shoot Khiron's mother's house up and make him come look for me."

With that, I watched Sadie switch back to the Hummer and pull off into the night. Although she'd just threatened my life, just the mere sight of her gave me hope. I knew I was going to do everything in my power to help her claim back the city: for Ray.

"Kings don't fucking die," I whispered up to the stars before I went inside of my shoe box to prepare for the street war to come.

To Be Continued . . .